Masquerade

Also by B. J. Hoff in Large Print:

The Captive Voice
Dark River Legacy
The Penny Whistle
Storm at Daybreak
The Tangled Web
Vow of Silence
Winds of Graystone Manor

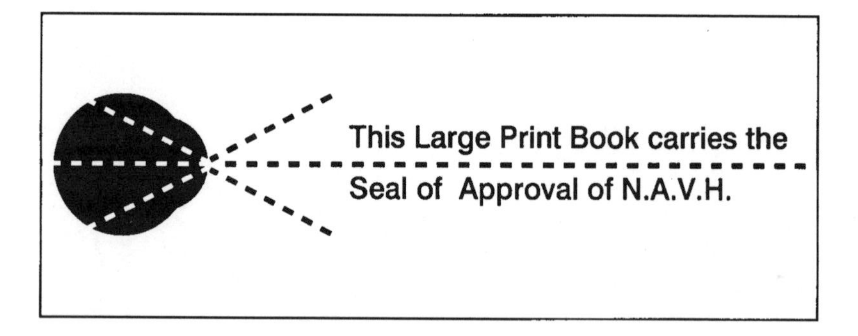

MASQUERADE

B. J. HOFF

Thorndike Press • Thorndike, Maine

Previously published under the title *Mists of Danger.*

Published in 2000 by arrangement with Bethany House Publishers.

Thorndike Large Print® Christian Mystery Series.

The text of this Large Print edition is unabridged.
Other aspects of the book may vary from the original edition.

Set in 16 pt. Plantin by Al Chase.

Printed in the United States on permanent paper.

Library of Congress Cataloging-in-Publication Data

Hoff, B. J., 1940–
[Mists of danger]
Masquerade / B. J. Hoff.
p. cm.
"Previously published under the title Mists of danger" — T.p. verso.
ISBN 0-7862-2376-6 (lg. print : hc : alk. paper)
1. Journalists — Alabama — Fiction. 2. Sheriffs — Alabama — Fiction. 3. Cults — Alabama — Fiction. 4. Alabama — Fiction. 5. Large type books. I. Title.
PS3558.O34395 M37 2000
813′.54 — dc21 99-058240

A faith that lives
in a heart that loves —
This can change the world. . . .

B. J. Hoff
from *Horizons*

One

Danni St. John had a white-knuckle grip on the steering wheel of the Celica. The dark night outside, distorted by a slanting rain and the hypnotic sweep of the windshield wipers, reminded her a little too much of an Edgar Allan Poe story. Any minute now she half expected to see a screeching raven come swooping down out of one of the enormous old oak trees that lined both sides of the street.

The radio wasn't helping. The only station she'd been able to pull in for the last thirty miles was apparently keen on *Phantom of the Opera.* With a tension-relieving sigh, she leveled her glasses on the bridge of her nose and nudged the accelerator a bit more, trying to ignore the edge of uneasiness that had been building inside her for the past hour.

The pavement was wet and lined with soggy leaves, so she shouldn't have been surprised when the car fishtailed and did a half-turn in the middle of the street. She choked off a startled cry as the Celica rammed to a stop. At the same time, a sharp gust of wind whipped through the trees, forcing bare limbs almost to the ground. Danni gripped the wheel even more tightly, flinching as a dazzling bolt of lightning nailed the street just ahead, bathing Montgomery Drive in an eerie luminescence.

She swallowed hard against the knot in her throat, then wiped her hands — suddenly clammy — on either side of the seat a couple of times. Finally, after a long moment and a short prayer, she scowled at her own skittishness.

"Too bad I'm not writing murder mysteries," she mumbled aloud, squinting through the windshield into the darkness. "Great atmosphere."

She could feel her nerves tightening, and the headache that had been relatively dull a few miles back now threatened to explode into a real skull cruncher. She hated driving at night, hated driving in the rain even more. The combination of both for over a hundred miles was taking its toll.

She checked the rearview mirror, then, slowly righting the car, began to inch forward. The welcoming blink of colored lights just ahead on her left brought a sigh of relief. She increased her speed a little, eager to find a place where she could get out of the rain, stretch her legs, and ask directions to the Colony. Her anticipation heightened when she saw that the multicolored lights belonged to Ferguson's Twenty-Four Hour Service Stop. Ray Ferguson had been on that corner for as long as she could remember.

She hadn't been back to Red Oak for almost five years, and even though she wouldn't have expected the sleepy little town to change much, there would almost certainly be *some* changes. Especially with the Colony nearby, she thought grimly.

The last time she had come home had been to attend her father's funeral. She had stayed only long enough to help her mother sell the florist shop and pack for her move to Florida, where she now shared a condo with Danni's Aunt Kathryn. She found herself hoping that her hometown *hadn't* undergone too many changes. A small town of no more than ten thousand people, Red Oak had never seemed to keep pace with other, more progressive areas of Alabama. In fact, Danni would have been genuinely surprised to find any significant differences in the town where she had grown up. Somehow she had always assumed that the tranquil little farming community, nestled in the northern part of the state, would simply remain the same.

Her brief spurt of cheerfulness abruptly

fled when she saw the lights at Ferguson's go black. *So much for twenty-four-hour service.* Her sense of expectation quickly turned to anxiety when she realized that the entire block was dark. Even the street lights were out.

She drove slowly through an intersection, now without a traffic light, and turned left into the service station. Another sharp flash of lightning provided just enough illumination for her to glimpse four youthful figures, garbed in white, appearing from the side of a white van parked at the pumps. As she watched, they sprinted to the shelter of the brick building's overhang.

Danni very nearly panicked. She slammed on the brakes, avoiding by mere inches the metal railing at the north end of the station's corner lot. The momentum threw her forward against the steering wheel, and she rested her head on her arms for a moment, breathing deeply until she could regain her composure.

She had never been a coward. The considerable success she presently enjoyed as a journalist and an editor hadn't been achieved by running scared. But the sour taste in her mouth at the moment was definitely *fear.* She was, after all, alone on a deserted street in the middle of an Alabama rainstorm, with no lights and no one in sight — at least no one she *recognized* — to reassure her.

With an unsteady hand, she wiped the perspiration from her forehead as she watched the rearview mirror. Her sense of logic seemed frozen. She couldn't decide whether to stay or try for a fast retreat.

As though echoing up from a dark chamber, the voice of the radio announcer now penetrated the silence. Danni vaguely realized that the music on the station had given way to a news broadcast. She found the smooth male voice oddly inappropriate for her present situation, then expelled a sigh of impatience with herself.

Her attention sharpened at the first mention of the Colony. *"Reverend Ra, administrator of the Colony, stated that Mr. Kendrick had apparently suffered from a variety of heart problems for some time. As a guest of the Colony, he will be provided with the traditional interment ceremony afforded to those persons who are without known living relatives."*

When the station resumed the music format, Danni switched off the radio, feeling as though she were suspended in some sort of absurd time warp. So intent was she on staying calm that she didn't notice the approach of one of the white specters until it tapped lightly on her car window.

She managed not to cry out, pressing a clenched fist against her mouth as she stared in disbelief at the apparition on the other side of the glass. The face peering in at her was ghoulish, frightfully misshapen by the rivulets of water cascading down the car window.

Danni's mind spun crazily as she tried to remember whether or not her doors were locked.

She dropped her gaze to the blue insignia on the left shoulder of the creature's jacket — a lotus imposed upon the outline of a pyramid, with a pseudo-Egyptian drawing of a hawk centered beneath it.

It wasn't until the bearded young man in the hooded rain poncho spoke that Danni felt the first stirring of understanding. "Ma'am? Are you all right?"

Danni stared at him, then glanced from the emblem on his poncho to the van. The same insignia — minus the hawk — was painted on the side of the vehicle. Feeling somewhat foolish and embarrassed, she loosened her rigid grip on the steering wheel and attempted a weak smile.

The young man outside her window studied her with apparently genuine concern. "Ma'am — is there anything wrong? Do you need help?"

Danni's fear now gave way to relief. She pushed her glasses up into her hair, their usual resting place, then lowered the car window. "I'm sorry," she said, her voice unsteady. "I suppose you startled me. The lights went out . . . and then I saw you . . . and I . . ." Her thought drifted off into the cold, damp air outside.

"Are you having car trouble?"

"No — no, I just pulled in here to get out of the rain and ask some directions." Her mind cleared even more. "You're from the Colony?"

"Yes, ma'am." The youthful smile was guileless, almost too serene, Danni thought.

"Then you *can* help me," she replied, studying him. "I have an appointment there first thing in the morning, and I need directions."

The youth's smile brightened still more. "You're joining us?"

Stuck for an appropriate answer, Danni considered her words carefully. "Well . . . yes," she finally said. "In a way. Say, let me park, and then maybe you'd be good enough to draw me a rough map."

He stepped aside, watching as Danni drove up to the side of the building and killed the engine. Before getting out of the car, she pulled on her raincoat and tucked her hair inside the hood. As she opened the door, the young man with the blond beard reached for her hand, and together they dashed for the shelter of the garage.

The three young people already gathered there — each wearing the same white poncho with the blue emblem — turned equally vacuous smiles on Danni as she stepped beneath the overhang. She smiled back at them. "Is the station closed?"

"I'm afraid so," answered the only female member of the group. She was an extremely pretty young girl, with shy eyes and lustrous black hair peeping out from the edge of her hood. She turned to the young man who had first approached Danni. "Do you think Mr. Ferguson is ill, Brother Penn?"

"No, I imagine he closed early because of the power outage," said the youth. He glanced at Danni and went on to explain. "The storm knocked out the power across town, as far out as the Colony. Of course, we have our own auxiliary generators, so it's really not a problem for us."

"We brought the van into town to get gas and have a tire replaced," another boy put in, eyeing Danni curiously. "Do you live here in town, ma'am?"

"She's coming out to the Colony tomorrow," Brother Penn informed them with the same pleased smile.

They were all young, no more than teenagers, Danni thought. The girl looked to be the youngest — sixteen at the most. The tall, lanky Brother Penn was probably the oldest, perhaps nineteen. He was the only one who wasn't clean-shaven, and the only one who wore the emblem of the hawk beneath the Colony logo.

They're just kids, Danni realized with dismay. She struggled not to reveal the hot stab of anger she felt. She couldn't afford to show a hint of her true emotions, not now.

"I'm sorry," she said warmly, "I haven't introduced myself. I'm Danni St. John. I'll be working at the Colony with the newspaper. I'm the new editor."

The girl was the first to speak, extending her hand to Danni. "I'm Sister Lann," she said shyly. "This is Brother Penn." She nodded to the boy on her left who flashed that same vacant smile that for some reason was beginning to irritate Danni. *I must really be tired,* she thought dryly, *when a smile gets under my skin.*

"And I'm Brother Rudd," chimed the short, apple-cheeked boy directly across from Danni. "This is Brother Hall — he's my life brother as well." His voice was high, almost childish.

Danni assumed he meant that the taller, dull-eyed youth standing beside him was his natural brother.

"The Colony's easy to find," said Brother Penn, who seemed to be the acknowledged leader of the group. "All you have to do is drive out of town on 72 for about five miles, then turn right at the old Suter Foundry on Dead End Road. But you said you weren't coming until morning. Where are you staying tonight?"

"My home is here, in Red Oak. That is, it used to be," Danni explained. "My mother retired in Florida, but some friends of the family rented our house until just a few weeks ago. They've since moved out of state, so the house is mine to use, at least for now."

The girl looked a little skeptical. "Don't you think maybe you should just follow us out to the Colony tonight, instead of staying in town alone? You probably won't have any power the rest of the night."

"Oh, no, I'll be fine," Danni insisted. "I've really been looking forward to getting home again."

And so she had. In fact, she could hardly wait to get unpacked, have a hot shower, and plop down on the high four-poster bed in her old bedroom.

"If you'd like," Brother Penn said agreeably, "give us a time, and one of us will drive in to meet you in the morning. You can follow us out to the Colony."

"Well . . ." Danni hesitated, caught off guard by their eagerness to help her.

"It won't be any trouble," he quickly assured her. "Just give me your address."

"De Soto Drive. Eighteen-ten De Soto — it's the last house on the right. A white two-story. That is, it *was* white. I suppose it still is."

"Great. We have to be at the bus station by eight-fifteen to meet some guests," he told her. "We could swing by for you afterward, about nine."

Despite her reluctance to accept their help, Danni felt that to refuse might arouse suspicion — and that was the last thing she wanted. "That's awfully nice of you," she finally said. "I *was* wondering if I'd be able to find the place, since it wasn't here when I left —"

Absorbed in her conversation with the teens, she jumped and whipped around when the high, shrill wail of a siren pierced the night. As she watched, a dark car suddenly bounced onto the driveway, seizing her and the others in the glare of its running spotlights.

Danni threw up an arm to shield her eyes, taking an involuntary step backward as the car cut directly in front of them and screeched to a halt. With the lights nearly blinding her and the siren still shrieking, Danni gaped incredulously at the dark-bearded giant who flung the door of the patrol car open and hit the pavement in one fast, furious movement.

Two

Behind her, Danni heard Brother Penn groan softly, then mumble, "McGarey."

"The sheriff," Sister Lann explained in a whisper, touching Danni lightly on the shoulder.

Danni stared with undisguised interest at the uniformed figure approaching. From some distant place in her memory, a glimmer of recognition surfaced, then ebbed, as she watched the man coming toward them.

Her first impression had been accurate. He *was* a giant. Of course, most men looked tall to Danni when viewed from her full height of five-two. Still, this one had to be at least an intimidating six-four. With shoulders broad enough to gracefully balance his height and an expanse of chest that would make most Olympic swimmers look positively wimpy, the man was nothing less than overwhelming.

She noted the roughness with which he parted the small group and pressed himself directly in front of her. Her hood slipped down and away from her hair as she removed her glasses and tilted her head for a better look. Her gaze traveled upward, then up some more, from the badge pinned to a dark leather jacket, past a thick, jet-black beard and mustache, finally stopping as she encountered dark eyes appraising her every bit as boldly as she was measuring him. For an instant her gaze flicked to the sable hair falling casually over his forehead, glistening like satin from the rain.

Danni's instincts told her that this big, somewhat menacing man didn't begin to fit the types of law officers with whom she was familiar. She had worked with a number of policemen, and generally found them likable and cooperative, but something about this glowering sheriff put her immediately on edge.

Deliberately, she forced a smile and was rewarded by a glint of what appeared to be surprise in his expression. His frown suddenly looked more concerned than hostile.

"Do y'all have a problem here, ma'am?" His voice was unexpectedly soft, with that sweet-flowing, unhurried drawl unique to Alabama men.

Danni had almost forgotten what a pleasurable experience it could be, listening to a gentle, creamy-rich baritone make an endearment out of *y'all* and a two-syllable word out of *here*.

"Problem?" She was appalled at the break

in her voice. "Oh — no, no problem!"

If it hadn't been such a ridiculous notion, she would have thought the man looked disappointed. More unreasonable still, she found herself feeling almost sorry for the young people he was scowling at with such open contempt.

"I suppose there's a real good reason why you're standing out here in the rain this late at night?" His tone was snide and directed at the youth called Brother Penn.

"Why, yes, Sheriff," the young man replied evenly. "We were hoping to get a new tire and put some gas in the van. But Mr. Ferguson has apparently closed the station and gone home for the night."

Turning his gaze back to Danni, the sheriff moved closer, apparently in an attempt to get under the shelter of the overhang. His dark hair now hung wetly around his face, emphasizing deep-set, disturbing eyes and high, firmly molded cheekbones that hinted of an Indian ancestor somewhere in his background. "And you are — ?"

"Danni St. John." Danni blurted out her name all in a rush, then immediately wondered why she felt so irrationally . . . *guilty*, as if she'd been caught in the act of committing a crime.

"You're with these people?"

Danni thought his tone held an edge of distaste and puzzled over whether it was directed at her or at the members of the Colony. Just as quickly, she wondered why it mattered what the man felt toward her or the others. Yet, she grudgingly recognized that she didn't want to be the target of his disapproval.

She was tired, she reminded herself. Really tired. Too tired to be rational.

"Well . . . not exactly," she replied. "That is, I'm with them, but I'm —"

"Miss St. John is the new editor of the *Peace Standard*, Sheriff," Sister Lann offered. "And she used to live here in Red Oak."

Danni looked at her, wondering if the girl had somehow sensed her reluctance to identify herself with the Colony. She hoped not, hoped she hadn't been that transparent, no matter *how* tired she was.

At the same time she sensed a sharpening of interest on the sheriff's part. In fact, he was scrutinizing her in a way that made her feel a little like a bug trapped under glass.

"The new editor, eh?" he finally said after what seemed an inordinate length of time. "Must be darker than I thought. I wouldn't have taken you to be out of high school yet." He crossed his arms over his chest, cracked a nasty smile, and added, "Ma'am."

I don't like you either, cowboy, Danni thought, suddenly infuriated with his redneck arrogance. But she simply smiled at him and said evenly, "You're right, it must be darker than you thought."

His expression didn't alter. "St. John," he said thoughtfully. "Any relation to the folks who used to own the florist shop?"

"My parents," Danni said coolly, meeting his gaze. "I'm a native of Red Oak." She watched him carefully for any change, thinking he might back off a little once he realized she had a right to be in what he obviously considered *his* town.

"I see." And that, apparently, summed up his opinion of Danni and her parents.

For a moment, he diverted his attention to Danni's car. "You're staying out at the . . . Colony, ma'am?" he said, turning back to her.

Danni didn't miss the slight emphasis on the word *Colony*. Puzzled by his behavior, she tipped her head to one side, raising her hand to brush away the rain falling from her hair onto her face as she studied him. "No. I'll be staying at my home — my parents' place. On De Soto."

He nodded. "The white two-story with the little greenhouse in back."

"That's right." Well, he obviously knew the town, she'd give him that much.

"No one's lived there for a while," he pointed out. "It's going to be cold. And you won't have any lights."

A lot you care, Danni seethed. "I'll be fine," she said sweetly through clenched teeth.

He shrugged. "Your choice." Still he continued to watch her, dropping his arms from his chest to push one hand into his back pocket.

Suddenly it hit Danni full force — the memory that had been teasing her since the policeman had first stepped out of the patrol car. *Logan McGarey!* Yes . . . it *had* to be! The high school football star who had joined the marines and eventually ended up as a highly decorated war hero in Desert Storm. *Of course!*

For a moment, Danni's past came rushing in on her, and she saw herself as she had been many years ago. A skinny, unimpressive little flute player with her middle school band, marching proud-as-a-peacock down the football field at half time, in a combination effort with the high school band for the homecoming game.

She had been no more than twelve then, and Logan McGarey an awesome senior and quarterback of the varsity football team. He had made local football history that night, staking his claim to the field and leading Red Oak to a stunning victory over their traditional rival from Huntsville. The team had captured the state championship for the first time in fifteen years. And, almost incidentally, the name *McGarey* had taken on its first real note of respectability.

The McGareys had been tenant farmers, Danni recalled now. They had been a large family — lots of children and relatives across the county. The family had never really enjoyed a good reputation. She seemed to remember that one of Logan's brothers had died in prison. There had been other scandals associated with the McGareys, but the details surrounding the circumstances had faded with time.

Strange, she thought, that the memory of that magic late-autumn night was still so vivid, even after all these years. Danni had fallen in love that night for the first time, watching the heroic senior control the football field in what was later attributed to both genius and an awesome physical prowess.

Bits and pieces of the past came back to her. Logan had attended her church for a time, she suddenly remembered. He had been tall and thinner then — a far cry from the big, thickly muscled man now standing in front of her. Back then, his clothes had never seemed to fit, and they had sometimes looked downright shabby. Logan had been the only one of his family who went to church — at least, that she knew of.

Her mother had commented on that fact once, and expressed sympathy for Logan McGarey. "You have to give the boy credit, coming by himself all the time. He must feel so awkward, attending church alone in those worn-out clothes," Nancy St. John had clucked sadly. "I wish there were some way we could help him."

Danni had forgotten about Logan, of course, once he joined the marines and left Red Oak. Even when he returned, widely touted by a number of state newspapers for his heroism, she had been too involved in her own whirlwind life to pay any heed to the fuss made over him. Besides, he had seemed light-years older than she.

Later, during the time when she was working in the Chicago area and free-lancing for some of the Christian magazines, her mother had sent Danni an article about Logan McGarey's wife being killed in a tragic incident in Huntsville. They had been married only a short time, and Danni still remembered how the article had wrung her emotions.

A sniper had opened fire on a mall crowded with Christmas shoppers. Several people had been injured, and Logan's wife had been killed instantly.

Abruptly, Danni looked up at him. *How awful it would have been for him. No wonder he looks so grim and unhappy.*

With a start, she realized that he had asked her a question. "I'm sorry?" she stammered.

"Your mother — how is she?"

"Oh — she's just fine, thank you. Did you know my mother?"

He nodded, and Danni was surprised to see his expression soften. "She used to stop at the service station where I worked after school," he said quietly. "And she always spoke to me at church. She was a real nice lady." He paused. "You look a lot like her."

His tone left little doubt that he suspected the resemblance ended with appearance. His voice took on the same rough edge as he went on. "If you're really going to stay the night at your home, I'd suggest you get on your way before it gets any later, ma'am."

He had a way of making a suggestion sound more like a command.

He turned then, raking a stony gaze over the young people, one at a time. Danni watched, curious as to the way his features darkened when he spoke.

"You can't do anything about your van before morning," he stated flatly. "And it *is* past curfew, people — you'd best be getting back to the Beetle."

"Curfew!" The exclamation escaped Danni before she thought. "Red Oak has a *curfew?*"

Logan McGarey fixed a dark look on her. "I'd imagine, Miss St. John," he said quietly, "that lots of things are different in Red Oak from what you remember — for a number of reasons," he added, with a pointed look at the Colony members. A muscle flicked at the corner of his mouth, and he lifted a hand to his wet hair.

"Pleasure, ma'am," he drawled, giving Danni a small nod before turning away and starting for the patrol car. But even though he slid his long frame behind the wheel, he made no move to leave. Instead, he simply sat there, watching Danni say good-night to the others. He was still sitting in the parked patrol car as she drove away.

All the way across town she puzzled over Logan McGarey. She wondered what accounted for his unmistakable hostility toward the youths from the Colony. They were little more than children, after all. And what had he meant about the "Beetle"? Had he been referring to the Colony?

She sighed as she pulled off Montgomery onto Leander, turning her windshield wipers on to high to fend off the rain that had renewed its assault. Idly, she wondered how long Logan McGarey would sit there in the patrol car. It was almost as if he'd been *stalking* those young people.

How could I have ever thought a caveman like that attractive? she suddenly wondered. Just as quickly she answered her own question, impatiently reminding herself that a twelve-year-old girl could hardly be held accountable for her romantic tastes.

It was several minutes later when she noticed the headlights behind her, and she wondered who else would be crazy enough to be driving around in a downpour this late at night. But when she turned off Leander onto De Soto and saw that the car was still behind her, closer now, she began to feel a little uneasy. She knew she was being foolish. She was in her own hometown, where the most exciting thing that ever happened was an occasional runaway cow stopping traffic in the middle of the street.

Still, it *was* awfully dark. And there wasn't another car in sight. Only Danni . . . and whoever was following her. . . .

She gave herself a firm shake. There was *no one* following her. Two hours on rainy country roads had made her a little paranoid, that was all.

Eighteen-ten De Soto. Even in the darkness, without the benefit of streetlights, Danni could tell that the house hadn't changed. It was still the same rambling old two-story with the ornate cornices and bannisters. The other children in the neighborhood had often teased her about living in "the gingerbread house," but she had never minded. She had always loved her home. It was big and showed its age in a number of places, but it was also filled with countless happy memories of the family who had lived and loved there.

She was eager to go inside and revisit her past. But her thoughts of childhood and the familiar comforts awaiting her were diminished by her growing feelings of anxiety. The car behind her had slowed down when she did, and was now pulling in to the curb just a few feet away. And the driver seemed to be in no hurry to get out. He was simply sitting there, in the darkness at an empty corner lot, as if he were waiting for Danni to leave her car.

Three

Danni gripped the steering wheel, forcing herself to take deep, even breaths. *This is nothing,* she told herself. *Probably just someone keeping an eye on a roving husband or . . . something. Whatever happened to Danni St. John, fearless reporter? Where's the old sense of adventure, kid? You're supposed to be launching an attack on yet another unsuspecting force of evil, and all you can do is sit inside your car and shake in your soggy shoes? Get it together, St. John!*

Slowly and very deliberately, Danni released the steering wheel, zipped her jacket all the way up, and squared her shoulders. She couldn't just sit out here in the driveway the rest of the night. Yanking the keys from the ignition, she pressed the house key tightly between her thumb and index finger, then scooped up her shoulder bag from the seat. With a determined glance out the window, she bit her lower lip and unlocked the car door. She took one more steadying gulp of air, then stepped out.

If only there were a light. Any kind of light. . . .

The porch was just a short distance away, but her legs shook as she ran. A sharp blast of wind-driven rain flung her hood from her head, drenching her.

She had almost made it to the bottom step when she tripped over a branch on the sidewalk, breaking her fall by grabbing onto a low-hanging limb of one of the old pin oak trees near the porch. She snapped another anxious look at the parked car, then took the porch steps two at a time. In her fevered impatience to get inside the house, she nearly jerked the storm door off its hinges.

She hadn't realized just how frightened she was until, trying to force the key into the lock, her shaking hands sent the ring clattering onto the porch. Uttering a low groan of frustration, she stooped, glancing toward the street as she retrieved the keys and straightened. On her next attempt, she was able to get the key in the lock, but the door wouldn't budge. Hunching her shoulder against the peeling wooden panel, she pushed as hard as she could, but the door held firm.

Her heart thudded to a dead stop when she heard a car door slam. Still, she refused to look anywhere except at her hands on the doorknob. She gripped it with a fury, heaving her weight against the door one more time. Catlike footsteps approached, and Danni willed herself not to scream. But when an unexpected circle of light pinned her against the door, she cried out.

"Need some help?" The voice was soft — and blessedly familiar. The tall, dark sheriff stood at the bottom of the porch steps, training a flashlight on her. There was just enough light for Danni to see what might have been a flicker of amusement in his eyes. But she instantly dismissed the thought. It was almost impossible to imagine this stone-faced colossus with a sense of humor.

Her relief quickly turned to annoyance when she saw his condescending smile. "I — I was just going in — what are you doing here?" She winced at the sniveling sound of her own voice.

He lowered the beam of the flashlight and took the porch steps slowly and easily, coming to stand directly in front of her. "Just part of the job, ma'am," he said evenly, looking down at her with an expression that now confirmed Danni's suspicion. Without a doubt, the man was enjoying this!

And indeed, Danni had to admit grudgingly to herself, she probably was worth a good laugh or two right now. Her hair was sopping wet and more than likely hanging in limp ropes all over her head. What little makeup she had been wearing was certainly long gone, washed away with the last shred of her dignity.

The sheriff was close enough for her to smell the wet leather of his jacket, and she noted with nasty satisfaction that he appeared to be as soaked and miserable as she.

"Want me to try that?" he asked, looking pointedly from the door to the key ring dangling from her fingers.

"It's stuck," she said unnecessarily, wiping a stream of water from her face with the back of her hand.

His expression was perfectly bland, but Danni still had the feeling that she was the target of his undoubtedly warped sense of humor. "Let me try it," he said brusquely, moving in front of her. He gave the key a quick twist and at the same time leveled a powerful shoulder against the door.

Naturally, it opened with no more than a squeak. Danni eyed his broad back with a mixture of disgust and relief, quickly donning a more polite expression when he turned toward her and motioned her inside.

"We'd better see if we can find some candles for you to use tonight," he told her, beaming a path in front of her with his flashlight.

"Oh — that's not necessary, really!"

Danni protested, entering the hallway. "I'll be fine now."

An unhealthy odor greeted them as he closed the front door and took her by the arm, keeping the flashlight trained on the floor in front of them. "You'll need candles," he stated matter-of-factly, beginning to guide her through the hallway. "An oil lamp would come in handy, too."

Seething at his uninvited takeover, Danni refused to admit to herself that she was grateful he was there. She *did* silently acknowledge the fact that his mood seemed to have improved during the time it had taken him to follow her out here.

"It was you behind me," she said.

"Hmm?" He flashed the light over the striped wallpaper, then motioned Danni toward the living room. "Oh, yes. Sorry if I frightened you."

"Why did you follow me?"

He looked at her for a moment as if she were some kind of rare fungus specimen. "It's been a dull night," he finally said. "I was restless."

When he would have continued to pull her along beside him, Danni stopped short, digging her feet into the one Aubusson carpet in the house, and glared up at him.

He released her arm, waiting. Danni

noted that he still looked faintly amused.

"Are you always this pleasant, Sheriff?" she asked, purposely lacing her voice with sarcasm.

He studied her, and for just an instant Danni thought he might actually apologize. But then he turned away and continued his search of the room. Danni tried to see the furnishings through his eyes. Her mother had been overly fond of ornate Victorian, and the room was a little too crowded with weighty pieces of furniture and a wild array of knickknacks, including a fat-globed oil lamp that Danni had always thought perfectly hideous.

The sheriff spotted a box of safety matches on the mantel above the fireplace and reached for them.

He handed Danni the flashlight while he lighted the oil lamp. "Let's see if we can find some candles in the kitchen," he said, already turning to leave the room.

By now Danni was feeling a little embarrassed about her shrewish behavior and hurried to lead the way. "You really don't have to do this," she told him, trying to keep the grudging note out of her voice. "Not that I don't appreciate it, of course."

He didn't answer. When they reached the kitchen, he placed the oil lamp in the middle of the big oak table and began to rummage through drawers beside the sink.

Danni took in the room with an unexpected tug of nostalgia as a whole parade of memories marched through her mind. There had been years and years of evenings spent sitting around that table with her parents. Somehow the kitchen had always been the gathering place for the three of them. Now the comfortable old round table, bare and showing its many scars, made the entire kitchen appear sadly empty and unfamiliar.

Lost in her thoughts, she didn't notice the sheriff holding the half dozen or so candles he'd found. "Okay," he said, glancing at her from his place by the counter. "These should do you, even if the power stays out until tomorrow."

"What?" Danni stared at him blankly for a moment, then recovered. "Oh — yes . . . I'm sure they will," she said vaguely. "Thank you, Sheriff," she added, trying to inject a little more warmth into her words. "I really do appreciate your helping me like this."

"No problem," he said shortly. "I'll get your luggage out of the car for you and be on my way."

"Oh, really, that's not necessary —"

He held out his hand. "Your trunk key?"

Before Danni could protest any further, he took the key ring and the flashlight from her and left the kitchen. His assistance would have been a lot easier to accept, she decided, if he didn't seem so . . . disapproving. Why, she wondered, had he gone to all this trouble for her if he found her so offensive?

It occurred to her that the sheriff's attitude might have something to do with the Colony. She hadn't missed his obvious antagonism toward Brother Penn and the others back at the service station. She shrugged. Whatever the cause, she couldn't do anything about it now. Not that she cared. After another moment, she took the oil lamp and started for the den.

The French doors were shut and apparently swollen from the dampness permeating the house. Danni gave the handles a sharp tug, balancing the lamp in her free hand. When the doors finally creaked open, it was to release an unpleasant, musty odor that made her wrinkle her nose and hold her breath.

She hesitated a moment before entering the room that had always been her father's retreat. Holding the lamp high and extended away from her, she took a cautious step forward. Once inside the room, it took her a moment to acclimate herself to the dark shadows that were only faintly relieved by the lamplight.

She saw the broken glass first, shattered in front of the gaping window behind her father's massive mahogany desk. Dazed, Danni stared for a full minute, feeling the cold wind pouring through the long, narrow opening where glass had been, watching the rain blowing in on the already ruined carpet.

Danni had a sickening sensation of destruction as she glanced around the room. The drawers had been torn from the desk and thrown aside, their contents spilled at random over the wet carpet. She was too stunned to make a sound until she looked past the center of the room to the floor-to-ceiling bookshelves and cabinets. The entire collection of her father's books, which her mother had reluctantly left behind because of the limited space in her shared condominium, had been ruthlessly tossed from the shelves. Most were obviously beyond saving. In the end, it was the waste, the cruel, meaningless waste of it all that made Danni scream. And scream again.

The sheriff, returning from outside, reacted by dropping Danni's luggage in a heap by the door, then hurling himself the rest of the way into the room. Deftly he blocked Danni's body with his own much larger one. Keeping her safely behind him, he pivoted, his gun ready, his trained gaze assessing the entire room in one sweeping glance. He focused briefly on the broken window, then backed Danni against the wall, still shielding her with his own body.

Finally, he returned his gun to its holster. His dark eyes went over Danni's face as he gently clasped her shoulders. "Are you all right?"

She wasn't. Danni tried to force the air from her lungs, but succeeded only in choking. Panic snaked upward through her, and she felt herself fighting for oxygen as she prayed for just one small breath. She clutched at Logan McGarey's jacket, managing to mouth a single word — *"Asthma . . ."*

His features went taut and he paled. The way his eyes darted over her told Danni he hadn't a thought of what to do. At the same time the familiar buzzing in her ears began, and a charge of nausea hit her midsection full force. She would lose consciousness any moment now.

The sheriff seemed to recover, bracing Danni against one arm as he bent to peer into her face. "Do you have medication with you? In your purse?"

With an effort, Danni nodded.

"Where?" he prompted her. "Where's your purse?"

Not waiting for a reply, he scooped Danni up into his arms and raced out into the hallway. When he spied her purse on the telephone stand at the bottom of the stairway, he carefully eased her, then himself, onto the bottom step. Danni was vaguely aware that his hands were shaking as he rifled the contents of her purse and produced her inhalator. She groped for it, but her hand was limp, as if disconnected from her arm.

"Open your mouth," the sheriff ordered, his voice gruff. The instant Danni complied, he squeezed the release tab, sending the liberating medication down her throat and into her lungs.

He watched her closely, drawing in a long, shaky breath of his own when Danni finally gulped in a swallow of air.

He continued to hold her as her breathing returned to normal. Weakened by the attack — the worst she'd had in months — Danni lay docilely in his arms. She was alert enough to feel surprise at his unexpected gentleness as he stroked her still-wet hair with a hand large enough to engulf both her own.

Even his voice had gentled to a low and reassuring drone as he studied her. "Better?"

Danni nodded. "Yes . . . thank you. I suppose it was the shock —"

"Does this happen often?" he interrupted. Those disturbing dark eyes plowed through the hedge of self-consciousness she had erected as a child against the despised illness.

Danni shook her head. "No. Hardly ever."

"Well," he said, his voice again turning rough, as though he'd suddenly caught himself stepping out of character, "you'd best get into some dry clothes, if you feel up to it, and I'll take you somewhere else for the night. You can't stay here now."

Danni frowned. "Of course, I'm going to stay here."

"Lady," he bit out, abruptly getting to his feet and hauling Danni up with him, "you *did* notice that someone broke into your house, didn't you?"

The scathing look of incredulity he settled on Danni made her cringe. At the same time, she wanted to slug him.

"I don't have anywhere else to go besides

the Colony," she replied with exaggerated patience. "And I can't very well go crawling in there at one o'clock in the morning in the shape I'm in. Not if I want to hold on to the job I just accepted."

As if he hadn't heard her, he turned her around toward the stairway. "You are *not* spending the night here alone," he grated in the drawl that now did nothing but infuriate Danni. "I have a few other things to do besides sit outside your house in the rain to make sure you stay safe and snug the rest of the night. You've had an intruder. You have a broken window. You have no lights and no heat. And you couldn't go out to the Colony even if you wanted to. They lock up the place tighter than the U.S. Mint after nine o'clock unless you make special arrangements for a pass."

Furious, Danni almost choked on her own words. "Well, then, *Sheriff,* just where do you suggest I go?" She was pitifully aware that there was no way she could manage even a semblance of dignity, standing there miserably wet and exhausted, her knees still shaking from the recent bout of wheezing. Nevertheless, she did her best to stare him down.

For one fleeting moment, Danni thought he was about to smile. A ridiculous notion, of course. He was obviously intent only upon humiliating her.

"Well, now, I know of just the place for you, *Miz* St. John," he answered softly, not a hint of emotion in his tone. "You can spend the night at the county jail. No charge, of course," he added generously.

Four

Three weeks later, seated at the stark white metal desk in her office at the *Peace Standard*, Danni replayed her first few days back in Red Oak. It would never have occurred to her that first night in town that, of all the surprises awaiting her, Sheriff Logan McGarey would turn out to be the biggest one of all. She could even smile now — at least a little — over her night in jail.

The experience was definitely not one she would care to repeat. The sheriff had been completely serious about her using the facilities of the county jail. Only minutes after she hurriedly changed into some dry clothes, he strong-armed her through the door of the aging County Office Building, handed her a ragged, suspicious-looking blanket, and pointed her to a sagging couch in a dark corner of his office.

Sometime later, Danni ventured a weak complaint about her discomfort, adding the observation that the office was inhumanly cold. Logan McGarey merely looked at her as though he couldn't quite remember who she was or what she was doing there. After a moment, he proceeded to offer her the alternative of a cell, if she would prefer.

Danni decided right then and there that she was in the company of an honest-to-goodness prototype of the Hollywood rednecked lawman.

The next morning he drove her home, allowing only fifteen minutes to spare before she was supposed to leave for the Colony. McGarey's only attempt at conversation was to ask if he could keep her house keys and look around while she was gone. Danni handed them over grudgingly, instructing him to leave them in the mailbox once he was done.

"You don't want me to do that," he growled. "That's the first place someone looks for a house key." He glanced at the garage and motioned to the light above the door. "I'll lay them in the base of that light."

"Fine. And will you also provide a ladder so I can reach them?" Danni replied blandly.

His gaze swept her petite form from head to toe, and Danni thought she actually detected a ghost of a smile. "Good point," he said. "How about under that shrub by the garage door?"

Since he made no secret of his disdain for her and the Colony, Danni hadn't expected to see him again. Brother Penn arrived as promised to guide her out to the Colony. Accompanying him, in the front seat, was a wizened old man with a cherubic smile and a pair of oversized glasses hooked around oversized ears. He looked, Danni thought, like a cheerful little gnome. Somebody's grandfather come for a visit, she figured. Or maybe another new employee — a handyman perhaps? Brother Penn had mentioned making a stop at the bus station earlier that morning.

She followed the white van out of town and onto an unpaved country road, which she vaguely remembered as the way to the Gunderson farm, then drove through a wide gate that looked to be recently painted. As she continued up a narrow lane that eventually wound through a thick grove of trees, Danni gasped with amazement at the scene that broke out of the mist-veiled woods. She was so intent on the futuristic setting, so unexpectedly stark and out-of-place in this rural area, that she very nearly crashed into the Colony van ahead of her.

With her first astonished look at the Colony facilities, she knew immediately why Logan McGarey had referred to it as the "Beetle." The domed building — brilliantly white in the sunlight, with a number of straight, narrow extensions exploding from the center — could, without stretching the imagination too far, be said to resemble an enormous beetle suspended in the middle of the field. The complex had apparently swallowed up the Gunderson farm.

A closer appraisal revealed two other buildings, also white but smaller and less impressive, situated behind the main structure. The entire scene was a study in uncluttered, modernistic architecture.

If the exterior had left Danni speechless, the interior was absolutely dazzling. Everything — *everything* — was white, including the walls, the cleanly designed furniture, even the plush carpet. Only the greenery in hanging baskets and an occasional touch of blue in the form of geometric designs on the walls added splashes of color. Each Colonist extended the decor, wearing a simple white toga, unadorned except for a blue sash at the waist and the embroidered blue emblem of the Colony, as well as an animal logo on the left shoulder.

Danni had soon learned that the Colonists were divided into ranks, each rank designated by the name of an animal. The highest rank, which seemed to function as the upper class of the Colony — and the watchdogs of the others, Danni suspected — was aptly referred to as the Hawks. These were the only Colonists granted any measure of freedom, as far as she could tell, and it was a minimal freedom at best.

Even Reverend Ra, the "Master Guide" and leader of the Colony, dressed in white: white suit, shoes, and shirt, set off by a blue tie. But clearly visible on the left breast pocket of his suit coat was the Colony logo — a blue pyramid with lotus insert and an embroidered scarab. His black, thick-framed eyeglasses were a dramatic contrast to his modishly long silver hair and beard. A tall man, he would have inspired attention in a regular business suit, but in his immaculate snowy garb, his appearance was indisputably commanding.

Other than the rather "creative" philosophy of the Colony, which Danni had almost at once recognized as a blend of Egyptian and Central American Indian mythology, the Colony followed a typical cult pattern. She didn't pretend to be an expert, but she had spent a number of months studying cult characteristics, and Danni saw no real deviation from the usual patterns.

Male and female living quarters were separate, and even the most platonic of relationships between the sexes was apparently discouraged. There was no marriage. Colonists abstained from alcohol, tobacco, sugar, and red meat. There were some fairly obvious signs of drug abuse, but so far Danni hadn't been able to gauge just how widespread it might be. Wisdom, enlightenment, simplicity, peace, and love — Colony style — were emphasized. The young people were entirely dependent on Reverend Ra and his assistants for all decisions. Names were changed as the members took on new identities, their lives centering around their spiritual family. Past ties — family, friends, schoolmates — were immediately and completely severed.

Most of the members were under twenty, although Danni had seen several elderly men and women on the grounds from time to time, including the little man — Otis Green — she had spotted that first day in the van. Clearly not a new employee as she had first thought, Otis always had a bright smile and a pleasant word for her when they met.

From all appearances, the students had no possessions, nor did they seem to want any. While she hadn't actually been all the way inside any of the living quarters, Danni had managed to sneak a few peeks inside the rooms. They were bleak, decorated in the predictable white motif, and bereft of even the most basic personal items. The only things the Colonists seemed to own consisted of the few personal hygiene items considered essential.

There was total and unquestioned obedience to Reverend Ra and the Hawks. Danni had already attended two "Faith Services," mentally noting the frequent appearance of such phrases as "be disciplined," "control your inner self," "reject the world," "yield to the light of peace," and other such nebulous slogans.

So far, she had seen nothing she hadn't expected, other than the elderly guests who were observed less frequently than Colony members and seemed to be exempt from most of the cult's restrictions. Dressed in everyday clothing, they appeared to be treated with respect and consideration. But Danni had not yet come up with any real clue as to their place or purpose in the Colony.

As she went on reflecting over her first weeks back in Red Oak, Danni realized again that Logan McGarey had been her biggest surprise. For example, when she'd returned home after her first day at the Colony, she had found her front door ajar, a glass service truck parked in the driveway, and, despite the chill autumn temperature, every window in the house open. She had raced through the rooms only to discover that a major cleanup had taken place throughout. When she reached the library, she found Logan McGarey, looking much less intimidating in worn jeans and a red sweat shirt. He appeared to be supervising the installation of a new window.

And, most surprising of all, he had actually *smiled* at her!

"I didn't think you'd mind," he said offhandedly. "Jed Curtis is a friend of your family, and when he heard what happened he offered to take care of the window right away." He paused. "No charge to you. He insists."

When Danni would have protested all the trouble he had obviously gone to, he cut her off with a casual, "No problem," then walked across the room to switch on a dehumidifier. As he turned back to her, he was smiling again. "I figured you'd rather not spend another night in jail, and I thought you might sleep a little better without the broken window."

Danni stared at him, unable to take in what he had done. "Everything has been cleaned up —"

"Not everything," he corrected her. "I just swept up and aired out the rooms. You still have a lot of work to do."

He had gone on then to apologize for his "bad disposition" of the previous night, pleading exhaustion. "I'd been on duty almost forty-eight hours without any sleep. Had a deputy down with the flu and another helping his wife have a baby. I'm a bear when I don't get my sleep."

Still reeling at the change in his behavior, Danni had somehow managed to stammer out her appreciation for his help. When she tried to pay him, however, his displeasure had been all too evident. To her own astonishment, she had ended up inviting him to dinner. More amazing yet, he accepted, then went on to throw her off balance by asking, with a grin, if she could cook.

Well, he would find out soon enough, she thought, finally stirring from her reminiscences. He was coming to dinner tonight, and she intended to pull out all the stops and show him that she wasn't entirely helpless. It was bad enough that he was probably dreading the evening. No doubt he had accepted only because she hadn't given him time to make a gracious refusal. A man like Logan McGarey — not that she knew much about men like Logan McGarey, she conceded — wasn't likely to be impressed by a quiet Italian dinner at the home of someone he clearly thought incompetent at best. He was probably used to more exciting dates.

This was not a *date,* Danni reminded herself irritably. This was nothing more than the . . . repayment of an obligation.

Just then Brother Add, her slender, sad-eyed assistant on the newspaper, startled Danni by appearing, seemingly out of nowhere. Danni jumped at the sight of him standing just inside the office door. She felt a familiar tug of compassion for the quiet, thin-faced teenager. The boy had a kind of "lost" quality about him, an almost pathetic eagerness to be helpful, that never failed to evoke Danni's curiosity — and her protective instincts. Add didn't seem to fit the same mold as most of the other young people. More alert, quick to respond, and obviously intelligent, he had already proven himself a valuable assistant. His talents seemed to extend from the creative to the technical, and Danni had quickly come to count on his help.

"Classes over?" she asked him now.

He nodded, giving her a shy smile. "Yes, Sister — Miss St. John."

Like most of the other students, Add seemed to have a problem with Danni's insistence on being addressed by her given name, rather than the *Sister* or *Brother* typically used by everyone else at the Colony.

She had explained to Add that she was merely an employee, not a member, and had encouraged him to call her *Danni.* So far, however, he couldn't seem to get past a rather timid *Miss St. John.*

"Reverend Ra wants to see you," he told her. "He said I should ask if you'd come to his office, please." As always, the boy spoke hesitantly, his uncertainty seeming to indicate that perhaps he shouldn't speak at all.

Danni sighed, then got up from her desk. She grabbed her raincoat before leaving the office. The *Standard*'s offices and printing facilities were in one of the smaller, detached buildings in back of the main structure. The structure wasn't far away, but the cold rain that had come and gone during the first week of her arrival had returned; Danni had learned the hard way that her asthmatic condition required her to avoid colds, as much as possible.

She hesitated at the door of Reverend Ra's office, purposely delaying her entrance. Her dislike of the big, florid-faced leader of the Colony hadn't surprised her; she had gained a fairly clear idea of what to expect during her research for the job. What she *hadn't* anticipated were the feelings of uneasiness and aversion that unfailingly accompanied any encounter with the man.

Few people intimidated Danni. She had grown used to going where she needed to go, doing what she had to do, all under the banner of faith in God's protection. But the Colony leader was an exception. In spite of his whitewashed, unctuous manner and self-righteous smile, Danni had felt an elusive but distinctly troubling sense of corruption about the man from their very first meeting. Even though she would have hated to admit it, he frightened her a little.

Finally, she rapped on the door, and he called for her to enter. She found him in a posture of meditation, standing in front of the wall-to-wall glass window, his arms extended straight out in front of him, his eyes closed as he mouthed some sort of chant. Danni started to turn and leave. But he motioned her with one hand to stay, opening his eyes and smiling kindly at her.

"Sister . . . come in, come in. I thought we'd have a nice chat before you leave for the weekend. Sit down, please." He walked over to his white desk — Danni thought nastily that he seemed more to *ooze* than to walk — and seated himself, gesturing for her to take the chair directly across from him.

"I've been wanting to tell you how pleased I am with your accomplishments so far," he stated, smiling broadly as Danni sat down. "I can see that you have the ability to make our little newspaper the vehicle I've long envisioned for the community."

Uncertain as to how to reply to his praise, Danni responded with a quiet, "Thank you." Reluctantly she kept her gaze level with his, fighting down the sick, cold feeling his stare evoked in her.

"I must admit," he went on with a chuckle, "that some of my assistants here questioned my judgment in hiring a young unknown journalist I'd never met."

His gaze sharpened, and Danni had to force herself not to look away when she replied. "I . . . suppose I wondered about that myself— Reverend Ra." She made an effort not to choke on the title.

He shrugged, raising both hands palm upward. "Your portfolio was simply too impressive to ignore, my dear. For one so young, you have been quite successful. I felt led to trust you." He gave his last few words careful emphasis. "Besides, it's rather . . . difficult . . . to find a competent person willing to take up residence in a rural area like this. Of course," he continued smoothly, "since Red Oak was once your home, it's only natural you would want to return . . . although I confess to being somewhat surprised, since you indicated that you no longer have family here."

"That's true," Danni said quickly, "but I always planned to settle here eventually. I'm a Dixie girl at heart, you see."

"Well, that's certainly to our advantage, Sister." His syrupy voice rankled Danni, but she had to admit the man *did* have a way about him. He might be as phony as a nine-dollar bill, but he somehow managed to exude a deceptive sincerity that his followers seemed to trust without question. She had already seen for herself that he was adored — indeed, *worshipped* — by the Colonists.

For her part, Danni wouldn't have trusted him with last week's weather report.

"I expect," he went on, his tone less saccharine now, "truly great things from you and the *Standard* in the future, Sister. We hope to move from our present weekly format into a daily soon, as I explained when you were hired. Naturally, I will be most interested in your progress to that end."

Danni shot a glance at him. Why did his words make her feel as though she were being warned? "I appreciate your faith in me, sir," she said evenly.

While it appeared this was her cue to leave, one unanswered question still bothered Danni. "If you don't mind my asking, I'm still not sure I understand why you decided to hire me, instead of training one of your own members to edit the newspaper. Brother Add, perhaps?"

It really didn't make any sense. From her extensive research, she knew that most cults maintained tight control over their "people" — not allowing them access to the outside world except under close supervision. She had already seen evidence of this. So why was *she* being allowed such free rein?

Reverend Ra gave her a thin-lipped smile, more a brief quirk of his mouth, and narrowed his gaze. "Let's just say we hope to project a new . . . image," he said, speaking carefully, as if measuring his words.

He rose and began to pace the room, hands clasped behind him, then pausing to survey the tranquil scene through the window once again. "Some of the townspeople seem to . . . question our motives. We selected you —" he turned his attention back to Danni — "to be our goodwill ambassador, our link with the community. As a more . . . objective . . . party, you can assure them that their doubts are entirely without substance."

Danni repressed a shudder of dismay. She suddenly felt uncomfortably like a traitor.

Reverend Ra returned to his desk, favoring her with an approving look and dropping his voice to a conspiratorial whisper. "Together, my dear, we can accomplish much."

Why do I feel as if he's licking his lips? Danni jerked to her feet, intent on ending the exchange as quickly as possible. "I do need to finish up some things before I leave. Will that be all?"

He rose from his chair, extending his right hand to her, just as he always did at the end of an interview. "Of course. You must be tired from the long hours you've been putting in this week. I'm sure you're looking forward to getting some rest over the weekend."

"Yes — yes, I am," she agreed. Anxious to get away from him, she offered a quick handshake then hurried back to her office.

Later, as she began closing up for the day, Danni was surprised to realize that a part of her was actually looking forward to the evening, to being with Logan McGarey. Almost instantly she wrote off the discomfiting notion to the fact that the company of almost anyone else — especially a strong and sturdy officer of the law — would be a welcome relief from the slightly sleazy ambiance Reverend Ra lent to a room.

Five

Exactly fifteen minutes before her dinner guest was due to arrive, Danni was already downstairs in the living room, waiting. She had dressed up more than usual for a quiet dinner at home, choosing a black silk dress with a beaded vest, even taking time to use a curling brush on her hair. In spite of her refusal to look upon the evening as a *date,* there was no denying the fact that Logan McGarey was an extremely attractive, intriguing man. And although he would no doubt exasperate her all over again, she was still looking forward to seeing him.

The doorbell rang five minutes before seven, and Danni wondered fleetingly if he was early because he, too, had been anticipating the evening.

When she opened the door, she was immediately thrown off balance by two things: the unexpected flicker of pleasure in his eyes, and the obvious effort he had made to look nice. In spite of herself, Danni reacted to both.

Although she made an effort to appear composed, she caught herself nervously rubbing the silky material at her neck. He stood there with an awkward smile, and Danni noticed how much younger he looked tonight. His black hair was neatly trimmed, as was his beard. A light blue crew neck sweater showed beneath his darker blue flight jacket. In his left hand, he clutched a lovely but unpretentious bouquet of fall flowers.

He handed her the bouquet as he stepped inside. "If this is an outdated ritual, I apologize," he said dryly. "I'm afraid I'm a little rusty in the social department."

Surprised by his words, Danni stared at the flowers for a moment before recovering. "Some things never go out of style, Sheriff," she assured him with a smile. "They're lovely — thank you."

"You know," he drawled while shrugging out of his jacket and draping it over the small desk chair in the hallway, "I *am* off duty tonight. My name's Logan."

"Oh — of course," Danni stammered. "Please, come in . . . Logan. I ought to get these into water right away."

He followed her through the dining room into the kitchen while she searched for a vase. "I hope it's all right," he said, "one of my deputies will be dropping off some papers later. I wanted to take them out to the farm tonight, but they weren't ready when I left the office. Do you mind?"

"No, no, of course not." Looking for something else to do with her hands, Danni lifted the lid on a large pan to peek inside. "Ah — do I smell Italian?"

"Yes. Do you like it? I'm afraid I don't have many specialties in the kitchen, and most people seem to like spaghetti —" Danni realized she was chattering and wondered what there was about this man that made her feel so ridiculously young and awkward.

"And just what are your specialties, Danni St. John?" Logan asked as he propped himself on a stool.

"What? Oh. . . ." Danni laughed lightly and shrugged. "I'm afraid about the only place I can hold my own is in front of a computer keyboard."

Nodding, he motioned to the salad Danni had begun to toss. "Want me to do that?"

Surprised, she hesitated. "Well, if you don't mind. I'll get the bread ready."

Danni was surprised at the effortless way Logan made himself at home in her kitchen, tracking down utensils and then loading them into the dishwasher after he'd tossed the salad. She learned quite a lot about him in those few minutes before dinner, and even more during the meal. The contrasts in the man were fascinating.

She discovered that he lived on a small farm; had an Irish setter named Sassy; enjoyed a wide variety of music, including bluegrass and gospel; was "addicted" to buttermilk; and had a black belt in karate. He was well educated, with a master's degree in forensic science and a specialty in toxicology. Why, she wondered, with such extensive training, had he chosen to stay in a town like Red Oak?

She was to discover that he was also an expert in the art of interviewing. Before they had finished their meal, Danni had revealed her weakness for chocolate cake, French fries doused in vinegar, and banana ice cream topped with roasted peanuts. She even admitted to a total ineptitude with appliances, an old aversion for instruction books, and a new fondness for Vivaldi.

She found herself laughing easily at his unexpectedly incisive sense of humor and warming to his casual, unassuming manner. They ate their dinner in comfortable conversation, Logan voicing an occasional accolade about the meal and Danni asking questions about what had been happening in Red Oak during her absence.

Later, he offered to get a fire going in the living room while Danni made coffee. He was on his second cup of what he referred to as "coffee with character" when he spied the Victorian dollhouse resting on a table by the doorway. He walked over to examine it, tracing the line of its mansard roof with his index finger. Dipping his head, he studied the miniature furnishings set in perfect order inside.

"This is really nice," he said admiringly. "I always thought that if I ever had a little girl, I'd like her to have one of these."

Surprised at the almost wistful note in his voice, Danni went to stand by him. "You . . . don't have any children?"

He glanced at her, then looked away. "No. But you know I was married. . . ."

She nodded. "Yes." After a moment, she added, "I'm sorry, Logan . . . about your wife."

He turned back, studying her. "You wouldn't have known Teresa. She was from Dallas." He bent down again to peer inside the dollhouse. "We met when I was in school there. We were married while I was a beat cop."

He smiled a little. "You would have liked Teresa. She was . . . special."

Abruptly, he seemed to shake off his mood. "Was this yours, when you were a little girl?" he asked, gesturing to the dollhouse.

"No, it's not that old."

He eyed her curiously, then grinned. "Ah — I know. You're still a little girl at heart, and this is your hobby."

"In a way," Danni agreed, smiling at him. "I built it."

He glanced from her to the dollhouse. "Really?"

Danni nodded. "My father used to make them. It was a pastime of his, and he taught me. I've built a dozen or so for relatives and friends. This is one of mine," she said, "but I have one in my bedroom my dad made. It's a Georgian style, much larger than this one. He won a prize for it at the state fair."

Logan's eyes roamed her face slowly. A flicker of something akin to amusement — but warmer — leaped in his gaze, then faded. "You're full of surprises, Danni St. John," he said softly.

He moved away then, going to the fireplace, where he dropped down to a large, worn hearth cushion in front of the fire. Danni made herself comfortable on the couch, curling up at one end with her feet tucked under her.

With his arms propped on his knees, Logan stared into the fire. "So . . . why come back here?" he asked without looking at her. "Why did you take the job at the Colony?"

Danni hesitated. She sensed that he was accustomed to getting answers to his questions, and the question was a natural one.

"It was a chance to come home," she began. He turned toward her, intently watching her face. His scrutiny unnerved Danni. She cleared her throat, trying for a firmer tone. "And the chance to actually edit a newspaper, on my own. Being a reporter is great, but the leg work gets old after a while."

Logan nodded agreeably as though he understood. "I'm sure it does. But I'm a little puzzled about something. I remember your parents as Christian people." His eyes probed hers. "Doesn't it bother your mother — your working for a cult?"

Frustration stabbed at Danni. She knew what this looked like to Logan, understood his aversion to her job. But she couldn't tell him the truth, not yet. She had learned in the past to cut her risks as much as possible by working alone and keeping her silence. This might well be the most dangerous set of circumstances in which she'd ever been involved. She didn't dare divulge what she had learned, not even to a policeman. Once she had the story . . . if she and Logan became friends, then she would tell him. But not now. For now, she would simply have to let him think the worst: that she had deliberately sold out, no matter how the idea repulsed her.

She chose her words carefully, turning to the fire instead of meeting his gaze. "I'm a Christian, too, Logan. And because I am, I suppose my work does seem — unusual. But it's just a job, after all. I don't have to accept the cult philosophy to edit their newspaper. And I *don't*."

She looked at him then, wanting to shrink from what she saw in his eyes — the disillusionment and what appeared to be a glint of distaste.

"Philosophy?" he bit out. "Is that what you call what goes on out there?"

It was impossible to ignore the note of incredulity, the bitterness in his voice. Danni steeled herself and went on the offensive. "And just exactly what *does* go on out there, Logan?"

The glint in his eyes hardened. "I'm not sure. Not yet." He stood, stretching his long, rangy form. "But I can tell you this — the place is rotten. They can enforce all the rules about healthy eating and clean living and peace and love and the *family* they want to," he grated, "but they're a bunch of crooks without a conscience, and the only *philosophy* they adhere to is greed."

Surprised at the vehemence of his words, Danni countered, "How do you know? Have you investigated them, or are you just making assumptions?"

He rested an elbow on the mantel and stood quietly, staring at her. "I can't prove anything, not yet. Right now, all I have are some seemingly unconnected bits and pieces — suspicions. But I *do* know there's something very wrong about the place." He stopped, studying Danni. "Why don't you go talk to Mike Harris at the *County Herald*? He'd probably put you on in a minute."

Danni had already anticipated that someone might eventually suggest this very thing. "Logan, the *County Herald* already has an editor. And," she added quickly, "an assistant editor."

He shrugged. "What about Huntsville? It's not that far away from Red Oak." He paused. "Why did you want to come back here anyway? What's here for you, without your family?"

Danni thought about his question for a moment and realized that, about this, at least, she could tell him the truth. "I love this town. I love Alabama. I always knew I'd come back someday." She gave him a small tight smile. "Why are *you* still here? With your education and experience, you could get a job with any law enforcement agency in the country."

Again he shrugged, returning her smile. "I suppose my reason is pretty much the same as yours. This is home. I don't really want to live anywhere else. Of course," he said dryly, "if I don't get re-elected, I may be checking out some other options."

"Is that a possibility?" Danni asked, surprised to realize how much the thought disturbed her.

He finished his coffee before replying. "With a political job, that's *always* a possibility. The fellow who's running against me in next year's election has a pretty impressive slate. And quite a following."

Danni frowned. "Who *is* running against you?"

"Carey Hilliard," Logan said, raking a hand across the back of his neck. "He's an attorney. Set up practice in town about two years ago. He's chaired a few important committees and seems to have some very influential friends."

"Are you worried?"

He drew in a long breath. "He makes me a little uneasy, I suppose. He just seemed to . . . turn up, you know, out of nowhere. Then all of a sudden, he's a real VIP."

Danni's next statement was as much a

surprise to her as it might have been to Logan. "Is there any way I can help?" When he lifted one dark brow in a questioning look, she explained. "I helped pay my college expenses by writing campaign speeches and drafting résumés."

He seemed genuinely interested for a moment, but then his expression sobered. "You might want to reconsider your offer. Hilliard is a real fair-haired boy with your boss, the *Reverend Ra*."

Stung, Danni fought down a harsh retort. "I am employed by the Colony, Logan. That's all. They don't *own* me."

His gaze burned through her. "Sooner or later, Danni," he said softly, "they own anyone who gets involved with them. Just be careful."

He pushed away from the mantel and walked toward her. "Let's change the subject, okay? I've been wanting to talk to you about something else." He sat down beside her on the couch, close enough that they could have touched. Danni felt slightly overwhelmed, as she had before, by his formidable size and disconcerting good looks.

"Can you think of any reason for someone to break into your house? Anything special they might be after?"

Danni looked at him. "No, there's

nothing here that anyone would want. Why?"

He pushed his hair back with one hand, then rested his arm on the back of the couch. "I found something the day I searched the house. It may be nothing, but I can't help wondering about it."

Danni was instantly alert. "What?"

"A scrapbook. I found it in the den. It had a lot of stuff about you in it — looked like something your folks might have kept."

Danni smiled and nodded. "I think I know the one you mean," she said. "My mother kept a scrapbook of me for years — ever since junior high, I think."

Logan still seemed troubled. "But it looked as if some things might be missing —"

"Missing?" Danni stared at him, puzzled.

He nodded. "On the last few pages, I think some clippings might have been taken — pulled loose from the tape. Do you have any idea what they might have been?"

Danni shook her head. "No, but I'm sure they were nothing important. Probably just college stuff. Where's the scrapbook now?"

"In the bottom desk drawer. With a couple of photo albums." He paused. "I'm surprised your mother didn't take that sort of thing with her when she moved to Florida."

Danni shrugged. "She left other personal things. She said she wanted me to have them." Rising from the couch, she went to the mantel and picked up his empty coffee cup. "Why don't you get the scrapbook while I refill our coffee? Maybe I can figure out what's missing."

Within minutes, he joined her in the kitchen, scooting a chair up beside her as he opened the scrapbook to the page where something had obviously been removed.

"Well, you're right," Danni said quietly, more shaken than she was willing to admit. "Obviously, something is missing. But I can't think what it would be." She glanced up. "Do you think this has anything to do with the house being vandalized?"

"I think it's a possibility, yes. You're sure you don't have any idea what might be missing?" he asked, gesturing to the open scrapbook in front of them.

"No," Danni insisted. "It could be anything. I'm afraid my mother has a tendency to clip every little article or picture even remotely related to my career."

Danni set her cup down and turned to find Logan staring thoughtfully at her. His face was very close to hers, and for one fleeting second she completely lost her train of thought.

"You were blessed with a very special family, weren't you?" he asked softly.

"Why — yes. Yes, I suppose I was," Danni stammered, surprised and flustered as she searched his face to identify the emotion she had heard in his voice. But whatever had prompted his question was already gone, leaving only a warm flicker of interest in his midnight eyes.

They both jumped, startled, when the doorbell shrilled. "That's probably Phil," Logan said, rising from his chair and following Danni out of the kitchen and down the hall.

Danni opened the door to a ruggedly handsome deputy in a tan uniform. His smile was lazy, his gaze curious as he looked from Danni to Logan behind her.

"Ma'am — sorry to bother you, but I have something for the sheriff."

Danni stepped aside and motioned that he should enter. Logan introduced the deputy as Philip Rider.

"Pleasure, ma'am," Rider said, removing his hat. His bold gaze lingered on Danni a moment before he turned his attention to Logan.

There was no mistaking the warmth of Logan's welcome, but Danni was puzzled by Rider's behavior toward Logan. Something in his demeanor almost hinted of contempt. Yet when he spoke, his tone held only courteous respect.

"Sorry to interrupt, Logan, but you said to drop this off."

Logan nodded, taking a thin manila file folder from Rider. "You checked the bus station tonight?"

"Just like you said. But no one came in. And I didn't see anyone from the Colony there, either."

"Then everything's quiet?" Logan said, glancing through the folder.

"The usual Friday night stuff. Nothing out of the ordinary." He looked at Danni. "I'd better get going. It was real nice meeting you, Miss St. John. Hope to see you again soon."

Danni shut the door behind him and turned to find Logan pulling on his jacket. "It's late," he said. "You'd probably like to get some rest."

For a moment he stood looking at her, his expression one of concern. "You're careful when you're out there, aren't you? At the Colony?"

His interest in her welfare pleased Danni more than it should have. "Careful? I . . . don't understand."

He frowned, but made no attempt to explain. Lifting a hand as if to touch her cheek, he instead dropped his arm back to his side. "Dinner was great," he said. "I'd like to call you. Tomorrow?"

It was a definite question, and, flustered, Danni hurried to respond. "I'll be here. I've no plans except to do some cleaning and laundry."

Then he was gone, leaving Danni to puzzle over him anew. Logan McGarey was as complex and unpredictable a man as she had ever met, at times an utter enigma. Fairly crackling with energy and an unmistakable restlessness, he conversely seemed adept at inspiring confidence and calm in others when needed. With a disposition that could turn from grim to genial in a heartbeat, he sometimes appeared formidable, just as often amenable. His strength and physical prowess were all too evident, yet Danni thought she also sensed a kind of innate gentleness in him, even a tenderness of spirit. Still, if he was vulnerable on any level, he managed to conceal it well. But then she had worked around law enforcement people enough to know that few were comfortable in admitting their vulnerability. Even the kind of unthinkable tragedy Logan had endured seldom crushed that iron control, at least not for long. It was that same control, she suspected, that often accounted for their survival.

As she went on trying to sort through her conflicting feelings about Logan McGarey, Danni found herself wondering what accounted for the cynicism that seemed to color most of his actions. Was he really as hard, as suspicious, as he seemed? Or did that flinty exterior merely mask a heart that had been too often seared, too deeply wounded, to let down its defenses?

Briefly, it occurred to her that her interest in the dark-eyed sheriff might be extreme, that she would do well to rein in her curiosity, if that's what it was — and it could hardly be anything else. On the heels of that thought came the even more unsettling awareness that in spite of his annoying ability to confuse and even annoy her, the room — indeed the entire house — seemed to have gone suddenly cold and empty in his absence.

Six

Danni had almost forgotten how even in November her home state could produce a deceptive warmth to tease the hardest of hearts with a subtle touch of springtime. This had been one of those days. By late afternoon she had become restless, enticed into daydreaming by the gentle sweetness of the day. And her daydreams, in spite of her efforts otherwise, seemed drawn to Logan McGarey like ants to a picnic.

She hadn't seen him for over a week, not since the night they'd had dinner together at her house. He had called her the next day, but hadn't asked to see her again. And she was hurt. Worse, she was angry — not at Logan, but at herself, for allowing the man to gain such a foothold on her emotions.

Danni knew she was woefully inexperienced when it came to romance. Actually, there had been no time for her to form any lasting relationships. Aside from one or two high school boyfriends, she had purposely distanced herself from any kind of commitment. Working part-time to help pay her college expenses, then maintaining a frantic career pace over the ensuing years, she had deliberately avoided attachments that held so much as a hint of anything long term. It hadn't been all that difficult; to date, she hadn't met a man who inspired thoughts of anything more serious than a casual date.

So her attraction to Logan McGarey was not only puzzling, it was downright unnerving. She simply didn't need any complications in her life right now, especially one like Logan. She had a job to do — a job that would ultimately demand one hundred percent of her. But the more she tried not to think about him, the more he seemed to insinuate himself into her thoughts.

It wasn't as if she didn't have enough on her mind. So far, she had found a frustrating lack of information — and no surprises — at the Colony. She had taken a few shots of the grounds, had even managed to sneak some coverage of the Faith Services. But what she had so far wouldn't even raise eyebrows, much less provide what she needed for a full exposé.

She *knew* the story was here. But how to uncover it?

The shrill chirping of the phone jarred her out of her thoughts. She tried to dismiss the stab of disappointment she felt when the caller turned out to be Philip Rider, Logan's deputy, instead of Logan himself. But her disappointment was nothing compared to her surprise when she learned the reason for his call.

"Dinner?" she repeated, already scrambling for an excuse to decline, then wondering why the invitation held so little appeal for her. Philip Rider was a good-looking, single man — at least Danni *assumed* he was single, since he was asking her for a date — and she had not been invited out to dinner for months. By all rights she should have been eager to accept.

Instead, she felt a vast relief in having a bona fide reason for turning him down. "That's really nice of you, but I'm afraid I can't. We had some problems with the press earlier, and I'm going to be working late."

"Tomorrow then? I'm off both days for a change."

"Well . . ." *Why in the world didn't she just say yes?* "I really can't. I'm sorry."

She heard a sigh on the other end of the line. "Can I try again?" he asked, sounding genuinely disappointed. "Unless that cousin of mine has you sewed up already."

Danni frowned at the receiver. "Cousin?"

"Logan."

His tone was light, but after she recovered from the surprise, Danni realized she heard a slight edge in his voice.

"There he goes, pulling rank again," he cracked.

"I — I didn't realize you were related," Danni said, feeling increasingly awkward.

"Yep. First cousins," he explained. "Though Logan has always been more like a big brother to me than a cousin. Hey, Danni — you're busy, so I won't keep you. But I *will* call you again, if that's all right."

Danni hung up after again murmuring a halfhearted apology. At the same time, a shadow fell across her desk, and she looked up to encounter yet another surprise. Logan McGarey was standing in the doorway of her office. He was in shirt-sleeves, his dark hair slightly ruffled, his aviator sunglasses resting low on the rather prominent bridge of his nose. He appeared mildly amused at Danni's look of surprise.

Startled, and entirely too pleased by his appearance, Danni wondered how much of her conversation with his cousin he might have overheard. "Well — hello!" she said weakly. *Why did she invariably seem to stammer in his presence?*

He removed his sunglasses, hooking them over the edge of his shirt pocket. "Busy?"

"Not really. I should be, but it's hard to concentrate on a day like this."

"It's a dandy," he agreed, walking the rest

of the way into her office. "How've you been?"

They made meaningless small talk for a few seconds before he finally sat down across from her desk. "I just had a nice chat with your boss. A real shmoozer, isn't he?" Logan's smile was still in place, but his eyes glinted with a spark of something unpleasant.

"What do you mean?" she said carefully.

He shrugged. "Let's just say that the *Master Guide* is also a master of evasion."

"I don't understand."

He studied her with a narrow-eyed gaze that made Danni uncomfortable. "How much contact do you have with Ra? Does he keep pretty close tabs on your job?"

Danni flipped the switch on her computer to turn it off, then leaned forward, resting both elbows on the desktop. Lacing her fingers together, she propped her chin on them, studying the sheriff with curiosity before acknowledging his question with one of her own. "Why do you dislike him so much?"

He looked away from her. "Cop instincts, maybe? I don't know." He shot a grin at her then, disarming her. "So — whose heart were you breaking when I came in?" He nodded toward the telephone.

Danni felt her face grow warm, wondering again how much he'd overheard. "It was . . . your cousin, as a matter of fact."

"Philip?" His smile remained in place, but Danni thought his voice sounded a little strained. "Well, now, he doesn't get turned down too often. He may never recover."

She laughed lightly. "Popular, is he?"

"You might say that. So he told you we're family?"

"Yes. I got the impression he may accuse you of pulling rank on him."

He grinned. "Only if I have to. I heard you say you're busy tonight —" He hesitated an instant, then continued. "I was hoping you might drive over to Huntsville with me. I have to pick up some papers, and I thought maybe we could have dinner on the way back. This is the first free evening I've had all week."

Danni was sharply disappointed, at the same time relieved to know he'd had a legitimate reason for not calling. "Oh. Logan — I'd really like to! But I'm working until at least ten tonight."

He frowned. "Why so late?"

Danni hesitated, knowing any discussion of her work at the Colony would only irritate him. "We're doing a special edition for tomorrow, and the press was acting up earlier. I have to stay until we put the paper to bed."

He crossed his arms over his chest, watching her. "Special edition?" he said, his tone casual, his expression anything but. "Why?"

Danni shrugged. "It's an anniversary issue. You know — 'Highlights of the Last Five Years' — that type of thing."

She shrank inwardly at the scorn that darkened his features.

He said nothing for a long moment, instead sat staring at the floral paperweight on her desk. "The *Standard*'s circulation is unusually high, isn't it? For a small weekly?"

"It's a good paper, Logan. And I'm not saying that because I'm the editor. Someone had already done an excellent job here before I was ever hired."

"I'm sure," he said, his tone flat. "I just think it's a little peculiar, all this community outreach stuff. Cults don't usually want to mix with the outside. They'd rather stay isolated, off to themselves, except for whatever they can bilk from the community."

He leaned forward in his chair. "A few of them publish in-house newsletters, but only for their own people — junk reading about the cult itself. Nothing like what they've been doing here. They're actually in competition with the *County Herald*."

"It's true they're trying to increase their coverage," Danni admitted. "I was hired with the understanding that I'd expand circulation and broaden the overall influence of the paper. What's wrong with that?"

"Maybe nothing," he replied with a small shrug. "But I can't help being a little curious as to what they're up to. Frankly, I've got a hunch they're after political clout, and the power that goes with it."

"And that bothers you?"

He leaned back in the white, plastic-covered chair that was almost too small for him. When he finally answered, he spoke quietly and evenly. "There's very little about the Colony that *doesn't* bother me. Very little."

"Well," Danni said with a shaky laugh, "I guess I know where that leaves *me*."

"Oh, I doubt that," he said softly. Slowly, he pushed himself up from the chair. "You're not going to work in here alone tonight, are you?"

Danni frowned. "No. Add will be here with me."

"Add?"

"My assistant. Add is his Colony name."

Logan nodded. "Is he usually conscious?"

"What is *that* supposed to mean?" Danni asked sharply.

"Well, in case you haven't noticed," he drawled nastily, "your friends around here are a little out of it most of the time."

Danni *had* noticed, of course, but she wasn't going to get into *that* with Logan. "You're not being fair. The people here are very . . . tranquil. Very peaceful."

"Very stoned," he said dryly.

The truth was he had only given voice to what Danni already suspected. "Stoned?"

"Unless you are extremely naïve — and I somehow don't think you are — you know exactly what I mean," he challenged. Without warning, he changed the subject. "Isn't there a lunch room or a lounge over in the main building?"

"There's a cafeteria, yes," Danni said, groping to follow his mercurial mind. "Why?"

"Are you allowed a break?"

"Of course."

"Fine. Buy me a cup of coffee." Then, grinning as though he enjoyed goading her, he added, "Or do they make coffee here? Will I have to settle for turnip tea or something?"

Danni stood up. "You can be a very difficult man, do you know that?"

Still grinning, he took her by the arm as she came around the desk. "That's one of the nicer things anyone's ever said about me, *Miz* St. John. You flatter me."

"Probably," Danni agreed.

As she sat across from Logan in the stark white, pristine cafeteria, Danni tried not to stare. All the same, she was keenly aware of his bronzed skin, the high, sharply sculpted cheekbones, and the almost black eyes. *Brave Eagle*, she thought whimsically.

"Do you by any chance have a Native American somewhere in your ancestry?"

The instant she blurted out the question, Danni cringed. She had never been known for her tact, but she usually managed to stop short of out-and-out intrusion. "I'm sorry," she muttered.

His eyes sparked with amusement. "I can tell you were a reporter before you were an editor. And, yes, as a matter of fact. My grandmother was Cherokee." He paused, and a faintly mischievous expression touched his features. "She was said to be a descendant of Tascalusa."

Danni pondered the name but drew a blank.

"Tascalusa was the chief De Soto defeated at the battle of Mabila," he explained. "The name means *Black Warrior*. Supposedly, he had black hair, black eyes, and stood seven feet tall." His eyes danced. "And he was mean. *Real* mean."

Danni lifted one eyebrow. "Well, they said blood tells."

He laughed, then took a sip of coffee. "So — you don't agree with me about the drugs? You don't think the folks around here seem a little . . . vacant?"

Danni glanced uneasily about the room, but it was empty except for her and Logan. "Actually, I'm not around the students — well, that's what they're *called,* Logan, stop scowling — all that much. I spend most of the day in my office, or in the press room. About the only time I see anyone besides Add or Reverend Ra is at lunch. Or when I take a walk around the grounds."

"Well, I'm no expert," said Logan, staring down at his coffee cup, "but I think I know when a kid's mind is being messed with. And I feel reasonably certain you've got a bunch of teenagers out here whose brains are being turned to mush." He glanced up at Danni, the lines of his face hard, his expression even darker than usual. "And I'm not sure that's all."

"What do you mean?"

"I don't know," he admitted, sighing heavily. "Right now, it's still a hunch." He surprised her by reaching over and touching her hand. "Just . . . be careful, okay?"

Danni swallowed with difficulty, managing only a short nod. His hand, nearly twice the size of her own, still covered hers. She cleared her throat. "You said you came to speak with Reverend Ra?"

"Routine stuff," he said, finally releasing her hand. "I need to locate any family members of an elderly man who died a few weeks back — a *William Kendrick*. Name mean anything to you?"

Danni thought for a moment. Then she remembered. "That's the name I heard on the radio — the obituary notices — the first night I drove into town. But, no, I haven't heard it since."

Logan's gaze went over her face. "It was the same with the other two."

"What other two? What are you talking about?"

He traced the rim of his coffee cup with one finger. "The Colony picks up indigents at the bus station and brings them out here, allegedly to provide them with food and shelter until they 'get back on their feet.' " His mouth thinned. "William Kendrick was the third such . . . 'visitor' to suffer a heart attack on the premises within five months," he said, glancing at Danni. "Doesn't that strike you as a little too much of a coincidence?"

Danni said nothing, and he went on. "All three were apparently indigent. No surviving family members that we could find. Not a credit card or a driver's license on any one of them. The first was found dead in the woods behind the Colony. They hinted at Alzheimer's and claimed he was known to wander off at night. The second gentleman died about six weeks later, found dead in bed in the guest quarters." He stopped, drew a long breath, and added, "And then Kendrick. He allegedly just keeled over while he was taking a walk about the grounds."

"Weren't the deaths investigated?" Danni asked him, feeling a little sick.

"Well, of course we investigated," Logan said, his tone tinged with defensiveness. "We did the best we could. The coroner examined the bodies, and I went over the death scenes. But the Colony objected to an autopsy for each of the deceased, and with no family to authorize —" he stopped, gave an impatient shrug. "It looked like a heart attack in each case."

"But you're not convinced?"

He looked at her. "Would you be?"

Danni shook her head. "What do you think it means? You're obviously suspicious of something."

He started to reply, then seemed to think better of it. Silence hung between them for an awkward moment before Danni broke it. "I suppose I should get back," she said, glancing at her watch and getting to her feet.

Logan nodded and stood, regarding her with a speculative expression. "When can I see you again?"

Danni was surprised by the question, even more surprised at how much she had wanted him to ask. Still, she managed to restrain her eagerness. "Well, I'm not sure —"

"You're working tonight," he said, not waiting for her to finish. "I'm working tomorrow night. That takes us up to Sunday."

Danni thought for a moment. "We could go to church, and then have lunch?"

He glanced away. "I don't think so."

Puzzled, Danni watched him. When he made no attempt to explain, she asked bluntly, "You don't go to church?"

The small muscle at his right eye twitched slightly. "Not for some time, no."

"You used to go to my church," Danni pressed. "I remember —"

His smile didn't quite reach his eyes. "Is this an interview, Miz St. John, or off the record?"

Danni felt the heat rise to her face. "Sorry. Occupational hazard, I suppose. I didn't mean to pry."

"But?" He waited.

"I was curious, that's all," Danni said, adding, "it's none of my business, I know."

His dark eyes revealed nothing, but his tone fairly dripped sarcasm when he said, "Doesn't the Reverend object to your going to church somewhere outside the Colony?"

"No one," Danni said, emphasizing her words, "tells me where to go to church."

He reached into his shirt pocket for gum, offering a stick to Danni, which she refused. "Somehow that doesn't surprise me," he said, his expression amused. "As a matter of fact, I expect no one tells you what to do about *anything*."

Danni merely raised an eyebrow and grinned at him. "Well, we haven't exactly answered your question, have we?"

"I think I've forgotten the question," he said, his eyes laughing at her.

"You asked when you could see me again," she reminded him.

"Right. How about if I call you over the weekend and we'll work something out?"

"Fine." Danni hesitated, then decided to just blurt it out. "Why do you *want* to see me?"

Before he could reply, she continued, her words tumbling out in a rush. "It's obvious you don't approve of my job. You don't like the people I work for. You don't trust anyone even remotely connected with the Colony. So what's your interest in me?"

His eyes met hers, and for an instant his expression sobered, grew almost thoughtful. But the amused glint quickly returned. "Could be I'm just cultivating your vote," he said mildly. "On the other hand," he drawled with mock seriousness, "it might be your chin. Without a doubt, you have the most stubborn little chin I've ever seen."

And with that he cuffed her lightly on the end of her stubborn little chin and walked off, leaving Danni, for one of the very few times in her life, absolutely speechless.

Seven

By ten-thirty that night, Danni was exhausted. But the anniversary edition was off the press and looked good. Everyone on the printing staff was gone, except for herself and Add. She gave him a wan smile, turned out the lights, and locked the door to her office.

"Your curfew extension is up, Add," she reminded him as they walked outside to the parking lot. "Do you want me to go in with you and explain?"

"Would you mind?" He gave her a grateful look. "If you could just tell my group leader why I'm late —"

"Sure." Danni rewarded him with a warm grin. "That's the least I can do to repay you for sticking with me tonight."

"You work hard, Miss St. John."

"I like what I do," she replied without hesitation. "My dad used to say I have printer's ink in my blood."

The boy nodded as if he understood. "Do your parents live near here?"

Danni was surprised at his interest. She'd been trying to open the door for more communication with the teenager ever since they'd met, with no success.

"No, they used to live here in Red Oak, but my mother went to live with her sister in Florida after my father died. What about your family, Add?" she asked after a moment.

He shrugged, glancing down at his feet as they continued walking toward the main building. "We don't keep in touch anymore. I haven't been home for a long time."

"Where is home?" Danni probed softly.

"Tuscaloosa."

"Slow down, Add. I can't keep up with you," she told him. "So — what was your name before you came to the Colony? Or would you rather I didn't ask?"

"No, that's all right," he replied quietly, immediately pacing his long-legged stride to accommodate Danni's gait. "My life name was Jerry. Jerry Addison."

Danni didn't miss his use of past tense. "Do your folks know you're here?"

He shook his head. "I don't know — probably not. They're divorced. I don't know where my mom is, and my dad wouldn't care where I am even if he knew," he grated out, still not looking at Danni.

"I'm sorry, Add," Danni said sympathetically, hearing the pain he seemed so intent upon hiding.

"It's okay," he muttered defensively,

glancing at her. A flicker of defiance sparked in his dark eyes. “I have a *real* family now — right here at the Colony.”

“You’re happy here, then?”

“Sure, I’m happy,” he said, a little too quickly, Danni thought. “You ought to join us. Everyone wonders why you haven’t.”

“I don’t think I could do that, Add,” Danni said. “This is just a job for me. I wouldn’t be . . . comfortable joining the Colony. I couldn’t change what I believe because of my work. I’ve worked in a variety of jobs, and each of them has been different. But my faith in God stays the same, always.”

He gave her a strange look, then darted a furtive glance around their surroundings. “But they expect you to join, Miss St. John. They’re going to think it’s strange if you don’t.”

“Add, my faith would never allow me to become a member of the Colony,” Danni said firmly. They crossed from the dirt path onto the sidewalk before Danni went on. “Add, what, exactly, do they teach you here about God?”

The boy shot a fleeting look in her direction. “A lot of things. They teach us about love . . . and peace . . . and doing good.”

Danni hadn’t missed the note of defensiveness in his tone. "What about Jesus?" she asked. "Do they teach you about Him, too?"

He looked away. "What do you mean?"

Danni stopped walking, waiting for him to stop, too. She had sensed the abrupt shift in his mood. He was no longer her cheerful, eager-to-please assistant. He had turned cautious, perhaps even suspicious. She framed her next question very carefully. "Jesus is the Son of God. Do they teach you that at the Colony, Add? About how He came to live among us, to show us what God is like — and how much He loves each of us?"

The boy made a short gesture of dismissal with his hand. "The Christmas story, you mean. I learned all that when I was a kid."

"Did you learn the Easter story, too?" Danni asked him quietly.

Finally he met her gaze again, but there was no mistaking the doubt and distrust looking out at her from those dark eyes.

"Did you learn about how that same Baby in the Christmas story grew up to be a Man, only to die on a Cross for the sins of the world? Yours — mine — everyone's sin, Add. That was the same Jesus." She paused. "Have you ever heard about Him at the Colony?"

She could actually feel the boy withdrawing from her. "I heard all that stuff in Sunday school," he said tightly.

"But you don't believe it?" Danni pressed.

"I don't — remember much about it."

"I see. So you don't talk about the Cross here at the Colony, then? Not at all?"

Danni already knew the answer. She simply hoped to plant at least a question, a glimmer of interest, in his mind.

He looked at her for a long time, and Danni could have wept for the doubt and the confusion — and the appeal — in his eyes. "Why would anyone do that? I mean, if it's *true,* why would He do it?"

Danni took a deep breath. "Because He loves you, Add."

The boy scuffed the toe of his sandal on the concrete. "You talk about Him like He's real," he muttered.

"Oh, He's real, Add. I promise you, He is *very* real."

"But He died —"

"Yes," Danni admitted. "He died. But He didn't stay in the grave. That's why I asked you about the Easter story. That *is* the Easter story — Christ's resurrection. He's alive today, and always will be."

"That's not possible," Add said, his tone

grudging. "It doesn't make sense."

"No," Danni agreed. "It really doesn't, does it? But then we're not expected to make sense of Christ's death and resurrection, Add. We're asked only to accept it, by faith, and to live accordingly."

"That may be okay for you, Miss St. John. But it doesn't have anything to do with me."

Danni saw the boy's haunted look, the pain of rejection and loneliness so starkly vivid in his eyes, and at that moment she wanted more than anything else to console him . . . to offer him healing.

"Oh, Add," she said gently, "it has *everything* to do with you! The Cross wasn't just for a few. It was for everyone. God's Son died for you as much as for me, Add. He loves you so much that if there hadn't been anyone else in the entire world, He would have still gone to the Cross. For *you*."

The boy stood staring at Danni with stricken eyes. But he had *heard* her, she was sure of it. He had listened. Closely. Suddenly frustrated by the overwhelming difficulty of trying to present the love of a *heavenly* Father to a child who had apparently never known the love of an *earthly* one, she breathed a silent, desperate prayer for the bewildered youth in front of her.

* * *

Later, after signing the group leader's information sheet for Add with an explanation as to why he missed curfew, Danni started out the door, longing for home. Her thoughts were on the leftover pizza in the freezer, her mouth watering at the prospect of pizza and freshly squeezed orange juice — her favorite snack. She would crash on the couch, eat, and read —

Then she remembered the file of advertising proposals she needed to review before morning. They were still on her desk.

With a weary sigh, she retraced her steps to the *Standard* building. It was almost eleven now, and the grounds of the Colony were in total darkness except for a few security lights scattered across the area. It was so quiet even the cool breeze that had blown up without warning sounded loud. Danni glanced up at the starless sky, surprised at how quickly the balmy temperature of the afternoon had dropped to a more seasonal chill.

By the time she again left her office after retrieving the advertising file, the breeze had become a sharp wind, and she began to jog the distance to her car. She was almost to the infirmary building next to the main parking lot when she heard voices coming from the front of the clinic.

She stopped at the sight of a small group of men coming out of the infirmary. Caution made her duck back against the end of the building to conceal her presence.

She could see a dim light glowing from inside, and a nearby security lamp clearly outlined the figures descending the steps. There were four of them, and Danni immediately recognized two as the orderlies who worked in the infirmary and the labs. They flanked the other men, both of whom appeared to be elderly — one, tall and gaunt; the other, quite short, with large, prominent ears. *Otis Green,* she thought. The group appeared to be headed toward the main building.

Without moving, Danni peered around the edge of the frame structure, her interest piqued by the lifeless, shuffling demeanor of the two men being escorted up the walkway. When an unexpected gust of wind came whipping through the towering pines behind the infirmary, one of the orderlies turned and glanced in her direction. Danni flattened herself against the wall, holding her breath. But he hesitated only a moment, then turned and continued walking, his white coat flapping in the wind as he mumbled a comment to the other orderly.

Once they'd entered the building, Danni hurried to her car and practically jumped behind the steering wheel. Something about the scene she had just witnessed nagged at her all the way home. After pulling into the driveway, she cut the engine and sat watching the house. The yard lamp cast a cheerful glow in front, while the night light beamed a faint welcome from within. But Danni's mood refused to brighten. She couldn't let go of what she had seen outside the infirmary. Could the men have been drunk, she wondered? She didn't think so. They had appeared more like sleepwalkers.

For that matter, had they actually been walking? Was it possible that the orderlies had in fact been *supporting* the two older men, that they hadn't been walking on their own at all?

She shook her head and opened her car door. Too many late hours were fogging her brain. She was exhausted, she was hungry, and she was cold. She would run through the scenario again tomorrow. Hopefully by then she would be thinking a little more clearly.

Eight

The house was cold. Danni went straight to the thermostat, grumbling under her breath, wishing she had left the furnace on.

Her hand on the gauge, she stood listening for a moment, instinctively on guard without knowing why. There was only silence, except for the loud sputtering and rumbling of the old furnace coming to life.

An instant replay of her first night home, when she'd found the den in such chaos, flashed through her mind. Yet everything seemed to be normal. So why was she having this sudden case of the jitters?

Taking a deep, steadying breath, she made a tour of the house, going from one room to the next, flipping the lights on and off just to reassure herself that all was well. By the time she reached the kitchen, she had found absolutely nothing. She was tempted to stop right there and put the pizza in the microwave. But she felt too grungy to do anything until she showered.

Fifteen minutes later, she had slipped into her robe — a creamy peach velour that her mother had given her on her last birthday — and was already feeling better. At her dressing table, she dropped to her knees, but as usual the hateful bottom drawer refused to open. With the last hard tug, it finally gave, almost knocking her backward as it yanked free. Grumbling, she retrieved a small cassette recorder hidden beneath a pile of lingerie. She pushed the top button for a quick battery check, then moved to force the cantankerous drawer shut, stopping when a small piece of silver metal caught her eye.

Danni picked it up, rolling it between her fingers as she puzzled over what it might be. She glanced from the piece of metal to the recorder, but nothing appeared broken. Getting to her feet, she held the metal up to the light for a better look, rubbing it between her thumb and index finger. Whatever it was, she didn't recognize it. Finally she dropped it into the pocket of her robe. She gave the drawer an impatient shove with her foot. Much to her surprise, it closed with a resounding bang.

Her earlier tension again surfaced as she began to pace the bedroom, speaking into the recorder as she walked. Hurriedly, she detailed the events of the day, concentrating on the unaccountable scene at the Colony earlier in the evening.

She crossed the room to where a stately Georgian dollhouse rested on a walnut stand near the window. Pausing the recorder, she nudged the floral drapery away from the window to look out. Startled, she saw the taillights of a car pulling away from the curb in front of her house. She edged to the center of the window, trying to get a better look, but the car was already out of sight.

Danni dropped the small recorder into the pocket of her robe and stood staring out the window for a moment. There had been no car within sight when she pulled into the driveway, she was positive.

Shaken, she moved away from the window. At the back of the dollhouse, she picked up a miniature porcelain doll in a frivolous lace ball gown from where it had toppled over onto the living room floor of the small house.

"Sorry, Cassandra, dear — you seem to have bumped your head," Danni said distractedly. Carefully, she returned the doll to its former position on the piano bench, where only that morning, in the throes of a playful mood, she had placed her.

At last she turned to leave the room, still puzzling over the car she'd seen, when a thought struck her. The dollhouse . . . something was wrong . . . out of place. . . .

She whirled around and walked back to the dollhouse, leaning over enough to allow herself a good view of the interior. It took her a moment, but she found what she was looking for. Not only had the doll fallen over, but in the bedroom directly overhead, a lamp from the miniature night table was on the floor, and a tiny platform rocker was lying on its side.

Logan hadn't been far from the truth when he'd accused Danni of being a "little girl at heart." The truth was that she still had a great *deal* of the little girl in her — at least where her dollhouses were concerned.

And that was what was bothering her now: the toppled doll, the fallen lamp, and the tumbled rocker in the dollhouse — they hadn't been out of place that morning. She was sure of it.

The thought of food was put on hold, her appetite forgotten. She wandered about the bedroom, her mind darting from one possibility to another, discarding each in turn. At last she retrieved the recorder from her pocket, along with the small piece of metal she had found earlier. Glancing from the metal to the dollhouse, she began to dictate a quick note into the recorder about the car she had seen pull away, the piece of metal she'd found in the drawer, and the out-of-place items in the dollhouse. She concluded with her suspicion that someone had been in the house during her absence.

That completed, she returned the recorder to its place beneath the neatly stacked lingerie in the drawer. Straightening, Danni turned toward the open bedroom door. If she didn't inspect the rest of the house, she would get no sleep tonight. But the thought of facing the cold darkness of the unused rooms made her stomach knot.

It took her a minute, but she finally steeled herself to leave the bedroom. She crept cautiously down the hallway, gently nudging the first door open and flipping the wall switch to bathe the room with light. She hesitated only an instant before stepping into the room and scanning its contents, sighing with relief when she found everything in order.

The room directly across the hall had been her parents' bedroom. She crossed to open the door, this time entering with a little more confidence. Only when she fumbled for the wall switch did she remember that this room had no overhead fixture. Swallowing down her unease, she considered going for a flashlight, but instead began to feel her way toward the enormous poster bed in search of the lamp on the nightstand. She found it easily, turned the key-shaped switch, and stood scanning the room.

Even in the dim light, Danni knew immediately there was something wrong. The skin on her forearms tightened as she took in the heaps of clothing that had been randomly tossed to the floor, the drawers of the tall bureau still ajar. Papers were scattered about on the carpet beside the spinet desk, and the doors of the double wardrobe stood open, revealing articles of clothing stripped from their hangers.

Danni's breath was shallow and coming much too quickly, her heart banging almost painfully against her rib cage. She spotted a piece of fabric trapped by the closed lid of the blanket chest. Wiping her hands down the side of her robe, she crossed to the foot of the bed and lifted the chest's hinged top. As she feared, the contents — what had once been neatly stacked linens and bedding — had been rifled and left in disarray.

Slowly, she lowered the lid and stood rigid and unmoving, listening to the sounds of the old house for something out of the ordinary. But there was nothing except the rumbling of the furnace and an occasional clanking of a pipe. She was wheezing and forced herself to pace her breathing, slowly and evenly, as she stared with sick fixation at the disheveled room around her. She felt the numb horror of violation, a sense of revulsion almost as strong as if her person had been assaulted.

Whoever has done this might still be in the house. . . .

The thought struck her with the force of a blow. Suddenly panicked, she lunged to close the door between her and the hallway. The old-fashioned keyhole lock below the doorknob caught her eye, and with shaking hands she turned the key.

She whirled around, her gaze going to the telephone on the nightstand. Her every instinct screamed to call Logan, but her pride and the need to protect her cover made her hesitate.

At that instant the phone shrilled. Danni actually cried aloud, then stumbled around the bed to grab the receiver.

"Danni?"

She could have wept with relief at the sound of Logan's voice.

"Danni — are you all right?"

"I — Logan? Hello?"

"I was getting a little worried. I called several times and didn't get any answer."

She wondered if he could hear the trembling in her voice. "I haven't . . . been home very long. I had to work even later than I'd expected."

There was a moment of silence before he answered. "Just wanted to be sure," he said softly. "I was worried about you being out there so late."

"Well . . . it's nice of you to be . . . concerned," she replied lamely. She hesitated, then asked, "Logan? You weren't here . . . earlier . . . were you?"

"At your house? No. Why?"

"I . . . saw a car pull away from the curb a few minutes ago, and I couldn't tell who it was. Not that there was any reason for me to think it was you," she added hastily. "I just wondered —"

"You couldn't see who was driving?" he interrupted.

"No, I'm not even sure where it came from. But it looked as though it had been parked in front of the house and after —"

"After what?"

Danni fumbled for her glasses, but when she didn't find them on top of her head, she stopped. "Nothing."

"Something's wrong." His voice had taken on the familiar hard edge.

Again Danni hesitated. But she could no longer stop herself. She had to tell him. "I think . . . I know . . . someone has been in the house."

"*What?* Are you sure?"

"Yes." She went on to explain what she'd found.

"I'm coming in," he said, not letting her finish.

"No, Logan! I just needed to tell you. It's not necessary —"

"Where are you?" he again interrupted.

"Where *am* I? Oh. I'm upstairs. In my parents' bedroom. But what —"

"Is the door locked?"

"Is — yes, I locked it. But —"

"Good. Stay put until I get there. I'm at home. It'll take me about fifteen minutes to drive in."

"Logan, I've been through almost the entire house, and I'm sure there's no one —" She swallowed hard, letting her words fall away. His clipped urgency had unsettled her all over again.

"Humor me," he said shortly. "Just stay where you are until I get there. Please."

He hung up without saying goodbye. Danni stared wordlessly at the phone, then replaced it with a thump. She glanced at the door, then down over herself. In spite of Logan's warning, she crossed the room to unlock the door. After checking the hallway, she hurried back to her bedroom — locking the door behind her — and donned a pair of jeans and a sweater. A glance in the mirror reminded her that she hadn't combed her hair after her shower, and she fleetingly wished she hadn't scrubbed her face clean of every trace of makeup.

Then she realized the inane direction of her thoughts and shook them off. As if her appearance was of any importance after everything that had happened.

She was dimly aware that she was still trembling, that her mind was groping to take in the events of the evening. At this moment, she felt the silence of the house and her *aloneness* more keenly than at any other time since the nightmare had begun. Silently, she willed Logan to hurry.

After what seemed an interminable length of time, she finally heard his tires screech outside, then the sound of heavy pounding at the front door. He yelled her name, then again, louder this time.

Danni practically yanked the bedroom door off its hinges as she flung it open and charged down the steps. He was calling her name for the third time as she whipped the door open. Mustering as much height — and dignity — as possible under the circumstances, she flipped a shock of damp hair out of her eyes and met his dark scowl with one of her own.

"For goodness' sake, Logan, you don't need to shout!"

Nine

Ignoring her, Logan pushed her aside and shouldered his way through the door. "Have you checked the whole house?" he asked tersely, moving toward the living room, flipping light switches as he went.

"Please, do come in, Logan," Danni said dryly.

Infuriatingly indifferent to her sarcasm, he tossed his leather jacket over a chair and kept right on walking, leaving Danni to scurry along behind him toward the kitchen. "How long have you been home?" he asked, not looking at her.

"How long? I don't know — an hour, maybe less."

He turned to face her, and it occurred to Danni that he didn't look quite so dauntingly large and nasty in jeans and a sweat shirt as he did in uniform, especially with his hair in disarray from the wind. Unconsciously, she swiped at her own tousled hair.

His eyes followed her movement. "What else did you find besides the mess in your parents' bedroom?"

Danni drew in a deep breath, anticipating his reaction. "Well — the dollhouse — the one in my bedroom —" She watched him closely for any hint of derision as she tried to explain.

But he simply stood there, his dark eyes holding hers.

"You see, I remembered where Cassandra — that's the mother of the dollhouse family — was this morning," Danni went on. "She was playing the piano. But tonight she had fallen onto the floor. And the rocking chair and a lamp in the bedroom were out of place, too."

"In the dollhouse," he repeated tonelessly.

"Yes. I know you probably don't understand this, but I always know exactly where things are. In the dollhouses, that is. I never seem to know where anything else is." She stopped to catch her breath, then added, "And there was the car —"

He nodded, and Danni was encouraged to see that he seemed to be taking her seriously.

"I could use a cup of coffee," he said. "Would you want to make some while I check the rooms upstairs?"

Danni could hear him walking around above her, thumping things and banging doors, and she found the sounds strangely reassuring. By the time he returned to the kitchen, the coffee was done, and she had scooped some peanut butter cookies out of the cookie jar and arranged them on a tray.

"Other than the mess they made, I didn't find a thing," he told her, eyeing the cookies.

Straddling a chair, he consumed half a cookie in one bite, glancing at the other half in his hand. "You made these?"

Danni was tempted to fib. Instead, she shook her head. "Thomas's Bakery."

He grinned at her.

She went back to the counter to get the cream and sugar. "I'm sorry you drove all the way over here for nothing."

He shook his head. "No problem," he said, helping himself to another cookie.

"I do appreciate it," Danni said, sitting down at the table across from him.

"Well," he replied, his expression still amused, "if I want to see you, I suppose I have to take advantage of the opportunities as they come."

Unsettled by the studying look that accompanied his words, Danni managed an awkward smile and reached for a cookie.

They traded small talk for a few moments before Logan's mood abruptly shifted. "So — can you think of a reason why someone would ransack your house?" He watched her carefully.

"No. Absolutely not." Suddenly a thought occurred to her, and with it a stab of fear. "How do you suppose they got in?"

"Easy," he replied. "Your bedroom window was unlocked."

Danni stared at him. "But that's two stories up —"

"With a monster of a tree leaning right up against it," he finished for her.

Dismayed, she stared back at him. "But it wasn't my room they tore apart —"

"I know," he said thoughtfully. "Maybe they got nervous and took off before they found what they came for. The phone would have been ringing off and on — I called several times. Maybe they were afraid someone would show up to check on you. But I wonder why they trashed your *parents'* bedroom?"

Danni was genuinely bewildered. "I have no idea. There's nothing in there except some old clothes my mother didn't want — her own, my dad's — even some of my things. And a chest of linens."

"Well, someone might just be trying to scare you, but I don't really think that's what this is all about."

"What *do* you think?" she asked, trying to ignore the cold touch of dread at the back of her neck.

"I get the feeling," he said slowly, "that someone thinks there's something here, something they want. Or," he continued thoughtfully, not looking at her, "maybe they're just trying to find out more about you." When he raised his eyes to meet hers, Danni was sure she could see the questions playing in his mind. "Are you certain there was nothing else out of place or missing?"

"No, noth— oh! Wait." Danni remembered the small piece of metal she'd found in the bottom dresser drawer. "I *did* find something, but I'm sure it couldn't be anything important."

"What?" Logan prompted her.

Danni told him, and he sent her upstairs to get it. When she returned, handing him the strange object, he examined it closely, rolling it around the palm of his hand. "Why do I think this is something familiar?" he murmured, holding it up to the light. "Let me keep it awhile, okay? Maybe it'll come to me." He stuck it down in the pocket of his jeans. "Where did you say you found it?"

"In my bottom dresser drawer."

"What else do you keep in there?"

Danni felt herself blush, not wanting to tell him about the recorder — or the lingerie. "Ah . . . nothing special."

He gave her a peculiar look, then grinned.

"Well, I think you need to be careful," he said firmly, his expression sobering as he leaned back and folded his arms over his chest. "And I want you to promise you'll call me if anything else happens — *anything*. If I'm not in town, I'm out at the farm." He ignored her attempted protest. "If for some reason you can't find me, get in touch with Phil Rider."

Danni was vaguely surprised to realize that the thought of asking Philip Rider for help made her uncomfortable. She bit her lip, hesitant to mention an idea that had been growing in her mind for days now. Still, the night's events seemed to offer a perfect opening.

"Logan . . ." she ventured. "In regard to my being careful — didn't you tell me that you teach karate at the high school?"

He nodded, lifting a questioning eyebrow. Danni took his cup to freshen his coffee. "I've been thinking that I'd like to learn how to defend myself," she said, returning with his coffee and sitting down across from him again. "Would you teach me? I mean, could I join one of your classes?"

For one long moment, Danni thought he was going to laugh, but he must have thought better of it. Still, his muttered "No way" brooked no argument.

"Why?" she countered. "I'll come to class just like anyone else. I'll pay you, of course. I don't expect any favors."

"*If* I were willing to take you on as a student," he interrupted, "you *would* pay. But the answer is no." He rose from the chair and went to stand at the counter, leaning casually against it as he faced her.

"Would you at least tell me why? I could learn just as quickly as anyone else and you know it."

His easy smile infuriated her. "Oh, I don't doubt that for a minute. That's not the problem."

Danni glared at him. "Then what *is* the problem, if I may ask?"

He took a long, leisurely sip of coffee. "I'm afraid," he said casually, "that with your stubbornness — and your temper — a few lessons in karate might turn you into a lethal weapon." He looked her squarely in the eye and grinned. It was clear that he was enjoying himself immensely. "I might be creating a monster."

Danni uttered a sound of disgust and hurled a look at him that would have withered a weaker man. Only when his smug expression gave way to laughter did she understand what he was up to. "You're teasing me."

"I was," he admitted. "But now I'm not. You tell me why you think you might need to defend yourself, and we'll talk about some lessons." His dark gaze was solemn.

"I should think you wouldn't have to ask," Danni said loftily. "Any citizen in today's world needs to know how to protect herself."

"Save it," he returned. "Just answer my question."

"I just want to learn, that's all," she fairly hissed at him. She could have shaken him for being so deliberately obtuse. "After all, *you're* the one who's trying to frighten me, with your warnings about being careful and calling you if I need help —"

"You could always get a dog," he said, ignoring her scowl. "Besides," he said, giving her no time to respond before changing the subject, "aren't you afraid of compromising your faith?"

Danni looked at him, unprepared by this abrupt change of subject. "What are you talking about?"

He shrugged, then explained. "Some people — at least some *Christians* — don't believe in martial arts."

"Why? It's just a method of self-defense, isn't it?"

"It is. But it can still come down to a form

of combat, if the situation calls for it."

Danni thought about this for a moment. "I don't think it's wrong to know how to defend yourself. Or to help someone else who's in trouble."

Again he lifted a shoulder. "Not everyone feels that way. It's a lot easier to plead ignorance — to do nothing."

Danni saw resentment flicker in his eyes, heard the edge of cynicism in his voice. "Why do I get the feeling you're talking about more than karate?" she asked softly.

Logan regarded her thoughtfully. "I probably am."

"Tell me," she prompted.

He shook his head. "I don't think so. You wouldn't agree with me anyway."

"Sometimes . . . I think you're awfully hard on people, Logan," she said carefully. "Does that have anything to do with being a sheriff?"

"No," he tossed back in an unexpectedly harsh tone. "It has more to do with the fact that I see too many people hiding away in their safe little worlds until something threatens their comfortable existence. By the time they start screaming for action, the battle's usually over."

Stunned by the unexpected force of his retort, Danni said nothing.

"Sorry," he murmured, avoiding her eyes. "We should have left it alone."

"Am I included in that generalization you just made?"

He delayed his reply only an instant. "Let's clear the air, Danni. I don't like the people you work for — you know that. I don't pretend to understand why you'd get mixed up with that bunch of —"

He made a dismissing gesture with his hand. "I don't *need* to understand. Who you work for is your business. But I *do* want *you* to understand something: the Colony —" his tone turned hard — "has changed this whole town, and a good many lives." He stopped, took a deep sip of coffee, and stared down at the floor for a moment.

When he continued, his voice was less strident but still firm. "They're up to some weird stuff out there. I can't prove it yet — but I know I'm right. For the last two years, they've been moving into areas very few people know anything about. They're making subtle little inroads into some very important places. Frankly, they scare me to death. That's right," he said, nodding at her look of surprise. "They *scare* me. They have, right from the beginning."

His eyes narrowed, and Danni could almost feel the anger burning from him.

"But let me tell you what bothers me a lot more than Reverend Ra and his little robots. This town is full of good people — many of them Christians — who sat back on their indifference and threw the city gates wide open to the lot of them. Only two families — who are no longer residents, by the way, their homes were burned down — went with me to the city council to try to stop the advance group who came in here and bought the Gunderson land." He rubbed a hand down one side of his beard; clearly, the memory still grated on him. "Rumor has it the Gundersons were paid three times what their property was worth. It was a private sale, and council refused to discuss the changes they made in the zoning restrictions to accommodate the new owners. I suppose the prospect of all that increased revenue for the town coffers — which has never materialized, by the way — was just too appealing.

"We gave up on the council," he said, his tone still edged with resentment, "and we went to the churches. *All* of them. We tried to tell them what these people were, what could happen if they weren't stopped. I did my homework, Danni," he assured her. "Before I ever talked with the first person in town, I made it my business to know what I was talking *about.*" He shook his head, and Danni felt the disillusionment he must have experienced during that time.

"You know what the churches told us? Most of them, anyway. They said they couldn't get involved. That it wasn't any of their business — it was for the city council to handle. A few of the people who understood wanted to make a stand. But there weren't enough of us. You really *can't* fight City Hall, I guess."

His attempt at a smile failed, and he went to look out the window across the room. "You know the saying: 'The only thing necessary for the triumph of evil is for good men to do nothing'?" he said, turning back to Danni. "That's exactly what happened in Red Oak. Everyone was so busy watching their television shows and going to Bible studies and fellowship dinners and committee meetings that they couldn't be bothered with anything else. So evil just moved in and took up permanent residence. The Colony got their land. They built their buildings and brought in their 'converts,' and their 'teachers,' and now they're bringing in their elderly 'guests.' It would seem," he said quietly, "that there's just no stopping them."

He looked at her again, but his expression

was shuttered now, closed. "We could have kept it from happening. Just a little support from the town leaders and the churches, and we could have beat them. Now . . . it's probably too late. And I hate that. Because they just keep spreading their corruption — more and more of it. They're eventually going to own the town — and the county, most likely. They'll destroy whatever is good about it and replace it with their own —" He broke off. "There doesn't seem to be anything I can do about it. Not now," he added, his tone weary.

He shoved his hands deep into his pockets and glanced around the kitchen. "You know, I love this town. And in my own way, I suppose I love the people. But I don't understand them," he said, shaking his head. "I simply do not understand how they could have let this happen."

Danni felt a little sick. "So you think I'm a terrible person for working there," she said, her voice thin.

He stood very still, looking down at the floor for a long time. When he lifted his gaze to hers again, Danni was surprised to see that all the anger and every trace of resentment was gone from his features. He wore only an odd little smile and a look she hadn't seen before in his eyes, a look that might have bordered on tenderness. "I'm afraid I would have a whole lot of trouble," he said softly, "convincing myself that you're a terrible person."

Their gazes locked and held. Something passed between them at that moment, something Danni had never felt before. Something that seemed to unsettle him as much as it did her. She fumbled for a way to break the tension. "This situation with the Colony," she said, "does it have anything to do with your not going to church anymore? Do you resent the people that much?"

For a moment she thought he wouldn't answer. When he finally did, his expression seemed to hold more pain than resentment. "I don't know," he said, knotting one hand into a fist and brushing it across his chin. "I just . . . don't know."

Danni felt an irrational desire to go to him, to try to comfort him. Fiercely, she suppressed the feeling. "Can't you somehow find a little tolerance, Logan? Even forgiveness, for the town? It sounds trite . . . but they're only human. People don't realize the damage apathy can do. Not until it's too late."

The look he gave her made her wince.

"You mean they'll eventually get it, maybe after some of their own kids have been destroyed by that —" He stopped, lifted a hand. "I didn't mean to get into this. Let's drop it, okay?"

Danni sensed he was right, that for now at least, they needed to change the subject. She cleared her throat. "About the karate lessons —"

He stared at her, then gave a short laugh. "I give. Be at the high school at four next Tuesday. The Thursday sessions are for teens only. But on Tuesday I'm starting a new class for the public. It's open to anyone who registers on or before then." He shot a quick smile at her. "And don't forget your deposit. Twenty-five dollars."

"How much for the entire session?"

He seemed to consider her question. "Well — let's see. Maybe we can make a trade."

"What *kind* of trade?" Danni said, immediately suspicious.

He grinned as if he knew she was expecting the worst. "Ten percent off the total if you'll write me a killer campaign speech. And," he went on, ignoring her attempt to interrupt, "*twenty* percent off if you'll have dinner with me tomorrow night as well."

Danni's mouth dropped open, but she recovered quickly. "The speech might be a possibility. But you said you have to work tomorrow night."

"I'm off at eight."

"All the restaurants in Red Oak are probably closed by nine."

"We'll eat fast," he insisted.

She might as well agree. The truth of the matter was she wanted to be with him. The question was *why*.

"All right. But, I want to be sure I understand you correctly. If I go out with you tomorrow night *and* write a speech for you, I'll get thirty percent off the total cost of the lessons."

"I didn't say that —"

"Oh, but you did, *Sheriff*. Ten for the speech, twenty for dinner. That makes thirty. Do we have a deal or not?"

He laced the fingers of both hands together in front of him. "I don't suppose you'd want to try for fifty?"

Her scathing glare brought a smile. "Right. We stop with thirty. I'll pick you up a little after eight."

At the front door, he turned back to her, studying her face with a peculiar expression, one Danni hadn't seen before. He touched one large hand lightly to her shoulder, his eyes searching hers. "Don't take any dumb chances, Danni," he commanded. "This business tonight bothers me a lot. Give me a chance to put it together, okay? In the meantime, be careful."

Her sense of challenge now waning, Danni couldn't quite bring herself to meet his eyes. "I'll be perfectly fine, Logan."

He gave her shoulder a quick squeeze. "I intend to make certain of that," he said before turning to go.

Ten

A strong rush of nostalgia assailed Danni as she walked down the hushed, tiled hallway she had known during her high school years. It was quiet now, but she could almost hear the clamor of lockers slamming and teenage laughter from years gone by.

After changing into the brand-new white *gi* she had purchased for her first karate class, she entered the gymnasium, her mood lifting somewhat. She felt a little foolish, appearing in front of strangers barefoot in the loose-fitting, drawstring pants and long-sleeved top that reminded her of pajamas. Nevertheless, she sailed through the double doors with confidence, prepared to toss a dazzling smile at the instructor — who was nowhere in sight.

Disappointed, she stood close to the gym wall, studying the other students in the room while she waited. The class was made up of about a dozen members, both men and women. Some huddled in small groups chatting; a few others were doing what appeared to be warm-up exercises.

One slender blond man, who appeared to be in his late twenties, walked up to Danni just then with a welcoming smile. He introduced himself as Logan's assistant and a science teacher at the high school. They made small talk for a few minutes, then he walked away.

Danni wished Logan would hurry. Not only was she eager to show him that she meant business by arriving early for her first session, but she hadn't seen him since they'd gone out to dinner on Saturday night. She had found herself missing him ever since.

It really hadn't been much of a date. Logan hadn't been able to get free until after nine o'clock, so they'd settled for pizza at Miller's, where they spent nearly two hours preparing an outline for a campaign speech.

Logan was not an easy interview. He seemed to think things like speeches and slogans were only for TV, and his idea of a platform was a piece of wood.

"Well, what are you *running* on?" Danni had finally demanded in abject frustration, wondering how any man who appeared to be so shrewd could possibly be so dense.

"A very low budget," he'd replied soberly, glancing up from Miller's Deep-Dish Supreme Pizza Delight. When she growled and threatened to make him wear his dinner, he had simply laughed at her. She had gone on to ask who would be the *victims* of this speech, only to learn that there was no intended audience. Logan simply wanted something ready, something to keep on file for possible use later on in the campaign.

"Ha! You are not running a campaign, Logan McGarey," she informed him. "You are designing your own deadfall!"

He had merely grinned while Danni fumed. Then he reached across the table with his napkin to wipe away a string of mozzarella dangling from her chin, which made it very difficult for Danni to continue haranguing him.

In spite of his resistance, she'd finally managed to piece together enough information for a rough draft. She had brought it with her tonight, hoping they could go over it before she developed a final copy.

When one of the gym doors banged shut, Danni whirled around. She tried not to gape at the sight of Logan, attired in a basic white *gi,* a black belt draped casually at his waist. Even though she felt conspicuously absurd in her own outfit, she had to give the man his due. Barefoot and all, he was impressive. *Very* impressive.

She watched him with guarded appreciation, waiting impatiently for him to notice her. She was certain he did — he looked directly at her. But when he didn't allow so much as a flicker of recognition to pass between them, Danni began to seethe.

So go ahead and ignore me, Brave Eagle — and write your own campaign speeches while you're at it!

Only once did she catch a glimpse of what might have been a smile in his eyes, shortly after he'd started them on their warm-ups — to "loosen the joints" and "stretch those rarely used muscles." By then Danni had decided that her joints were permanently cemented and that a number of her muscles had *never* been used.

Danni prided herself on being in reasonably good shape. She wasn't a runner, and she wasn't big on any particular form of physical fitness, but she did walk often, occasionally went to the club, and kept her weight within two or three pounds of what it was supposed to be. At the moment, however, she felt more like a glob of stale glue. Her only consolation was that very few of the others in the class appeared to be faring any better than she.

Only their tall, dark *sensei* — the Japanese title for teacher, which Logan employed during the session — seemed to be at ease and obviously enjoying himself as he presided over this brutal misuse of the human body. He and his assistant, Mark Clifford, weren't even breathing hard as they participated in the warm-ups.

Danni spitefully decided to ask Logan later how a man *his age* endured this kind of punishment. However, she grudgingly reminded herself that this was, after all, her own idea, and Logan was only doing what he was paid to do — and doing it very well. So she set about getting her money's worth. Even so, she nearly groaned aloud at the thought that she hadn't even made it past the preliminary stuff yet.

By the time they finally reached the end of the leg stretches and sit-ups, Danni was convinced that she had been insane. This was not for her. She had come with the intention of learning to defend herself, and instead she was killing herself. The only thing that kept her from walking — no, *running* — out of the gym was the knowledge that she would eventually have to face Logan again. So she stayed.

She stayed and was initiated into the techniques of the attention stance and the horseback stance and the cat stance. She learned about high blocks and low blocks and middle blocks. She practiced the karate shout, deciding it was easily the most manageable technique among all this craziness, and it gave her some nasty little sense of satisfaction to use it every time Logan came close to her. She was also given a first-hand demonstration of punches and strikes, front kicks and side kicks, high kicks and round kicks and elbow attacks. Above all she began to understand pain, real physical pain: galvanizing, agonizing neck pain and back pain and leg pain.

She refused to acknowledge to herself that the sudden acceleration of her heartbeat when Logan gently encircled her waist with his large hands to demonstrate how to bend and block had anything to do with his nearness or his touch. After all, she was exhausted, wasn't she? The thundering pulse she seemed to have developed was most likely the result of extreme fatigue and utter frustration.

Just before the class was about to end, Logan brought the activity to a halt and began to speak. Danni was struck, not for the first time, by the inescapable magnetism of the man. He seemed to charge the very air with a sharp current of energy. As she had in the past, she wondered about this enigma of a man who could, she suspected, cower the hardest of criminals, yet at the least likely moment reveal an unexpected gentleness.

Her own reaction to him puzzled her every bit as much as his attitude toward *her*. Much of the time she considered thumping him on the head. But there were those rare disturbing moments when she warmed to the smile in his eyes and delighted in his soft, deep-pitched laugh or his fleeting touch on her shoulder.

She wasn't so sure but what Logan didn't have his own share of conflicting feelings. Admittedly, his behavior toward her was most often that of indulgent amusement. But every now and then Danni would catch him watching her with an expression that hinted at some disconcerting depth of feeling.

It should worry her, she supposed, that lately she'd even found herself reading a touch of tenderness into his condescending sneer.

Logan's words pulled her back to her surroundings. "You already know that *karate* means 'open hand,' " he was saying. "This class will stress defense only. My reason for working with you is not to teach you to inflict pain on another person, but to keep you from becoming a victim."

His gaze narrowed slightly as he went on. "You need to remember one thing. Reaction is all-important with karate — just as it is with a lot of other things in life. You wait too long, and you lose the moment. There's a point in time when you have the advantage, when you have the opportunity to overcome." His stare was hard and commanding as he made deliberate eye contact, one by one, with each person in the room, and Danni knew that, as had been the case that night in the kitchen, he was referring to more than karate. "If you don't react when you should, if you wait too long, then you invite defeat."

After a noticeable pause he added, "Sometimes, you can't avoid confrontation. That's when it's essential that you make the right choices, at exactly the right time. Hopefully, this class will help you learn how to do that."

His tone lightened abruptly. "Earlier this evening, some of you requested a demonstration. If you like, Mark and I will run through a few brief techniques before you leave."

It occurred to Danni, as she watched the two men bow to each other and begin their exhibition, that Logan, with all his rhythmic grace and fluid movement, could undeniably become a lethal weapon once unleashed.

She stood unmoving, watching the two throw lightning-quick punches, blocking expertly with perfect balance. The dull *thwack* of their blows echoed through the gym. The ends of Logan's black belt swirled loosely about his lean waist as his movements grew faster, his hands slicing the air with almost invisible strikes, his powerful shoulders tightening and easing beneath the white material, his long legs dancing in a flowing but unpredictable pattern of finesse.

Her irritation with him disappeared, giving way to admiration and still another unfamiliar emotion that threatened to undo her when, the demonstration ended and the class dismissed, he finally approached her.

"Cute," he said dryly, his eyes twinkling as he assessed Danni from head to toe. "You look about fourteen in that *gi*, Halfpint."

"Believe me, *sensei*," Danni grated nastily, "I feel a lot more than fourteen right now! More like a hundred."

"Ah," he drawled with patently fake concern, "suffering, are you?"

"Would you really like to know how I feel, Logan?"

He laughed. "I think I'm familiar with most of the standard complaints. Just wait till tomorrow morning — it gets worse."

She groaned. "Maybe I should just buy a dog, like you suggested."

"You're not going to give up that easily?" he countered.

"I'll let you know tomorrow."

He touched her shoulder. "I've been meaning to ask you . . . do you have plans for Thanksgiving Day?"

"Thanksgiving Day?" Danni repeated, frowning slightly.

"It's day after tomorrow, remember?" He smiled at her obvious lapse of memory.

Danni lightly smacked the side of her head with the open palm of one hand. "I can't *believe* I'd forget something like that!"

"Good, then you're free. I thought maybe you could come out to the farm and have dinner with Tucker and me."

"Tucker?"

"Oh, that's right — you haven't met Tucker yet, have you? Tucker Wells. He's what the old plantation owners would have called an overseer, I suppose. 'Course, I don't have a plantation — just a little farm — so I'm not sure what his title is. But he takes care of the place for me. Does a little of everything, including the cooking. Otherwise, I'd probably starve." Another thought seemed to strike him, and his smile widened. "Listen — would you really like to have a dog?"

Danni stared at him for a moment. "A dog — well, sure, I guess. I've thought about it. Could I forget the karate lessons if I bought a dog?"

He shook his head in mock disillusionment. "I'm surprised at you. Do you know," he said, a glimmer of mischief lighting his eyes, "that there's a ninety-year-old lady in the Midwest who recently earned her black belt?"

Danni hesitated only a moment, then fanned her eyelashes ingenuously. "That's a great idea, *sensei*," she cooed. "I'll come back in sixty-three years, okay?"

He laughed delightedly. "About the dog. Sassy — she's my Irish setter — had eight puppies a couple of weeks ago. If you'd really like to have a dog, you can pick out the one you want Thursday, and when it's weaned, it's all yours." He grinned. "They're good Irish stock, I guarantee it."

"Mmm. Like you, I suppose."

His smile weakened unaccountably, and he glanced away from her. "If you want to take advantage of the showers, they're in there," he said flatly, pointing to a door behind Danni.

Surprised by the sudden change in him,

Danni nodded. "I know, I went to school here. About Thanksgiving — I'd love to come, if you're serious. What can I bring?"

"Absolutely nothing but yourself," he said, his smile returning. "But I'll come and get you, so you don't have to drive back alone that night. We probably won't eat until after six."

"Oh, you don't have to do that. I'm used to driving in alone from the Colony —"

"I'll pick you up at five," he said in a tone that clearly meant to close the conversation.

Eleven

This was still another side of Logan, this playful mood, Danni realized. On his knees beside the lovely, mahogany setter and her frisky pups, he looked comfortable and relaxed in worn jeans and a flannel shirt. As he picked up one squirming, copper-colored puppy after another for Danni's inspection, he smiled over each one like a proud father.

She haggled over her decision so long that Logan finally uttered a sound of disgust. "I always thought a puppy was a puppy, didn't you, Tucker? Seems I was wrong."

His words were directed to the silver-haired man standing nearby — Tucker Wells.

Tucker smiled at Danni, and she was again taken with the inherent kindness of the man's face.

On their way out to the farm for Thanksgiving dinner, Logan had told her a little about his friend. Tucker was an ex-SWAT sergeant from Dallas who had befriended Logan as a street cop fresh out of the academy.

Apparently, the older man had been seriously injured during a drug bust years before — not long after the death of Logan's wife, Teresa. Tucker had been forced to take disability retirement, and Logan, reluctant to stay in the home he had shared with Teresa, had purchased this farm and convinced his friend to move in and help him manage the place.

The arrangement, according to Logan, had turned out to be a good one for both of them. He explained that Tucker was a "genius at organization," keeping the farm running smoothly and "keeping me in line as well."

Danni couldn't imagine anyone keeping Logan "in line," but after an hour in the presence of Tucker Wells, she decided that the former policeman probably could do just that. An intriguing man who looked far more like a middle-aged college professor than a former SWAT cop, he possessed a soft Texas drawl and an unmistakable dry wit. Slender with patrician features, his shining silver hair and wire-framed eyeglasses worked together to give him a dignified, almost genteel appearance, even in his rough work clothes. Danni had liked him immediately.

He went on smiling at her as she continued to fuss over the puppies. Finally, she scooped up the darkest and the smallest of the litter. He wriggled and thrashed his sturdy little legs, then plopped a large wet kiss on the end of Danni's nose.

"This one," she announced with conviction.

Logan looked surprised. "That's the runt of the litter, though he seems to think he's the boss of the bunch."

"Logan named him 'Chief' the day after he was born," Tucker said, chuckling. "Thinks he's real tough, that one does."

"The runt, huh?" Danni said, glancing at Logan, who was still watching her with the puppy.

"Just like you, Half-pint," he cracked.

"Nope," she countered. "I *was* the litter. An only child."

"Spoiled?"

"Is that a question or an observation?"

A slow grin was his only reply.

"What about you?" she asked Logan. "And don't tell me *you* were the runt!"

Tucker laughed at their banter, but Logan's smile had dimmed by the time he got to his feet. "No," he said shortly. "I was the oldest and the biggest."

"Of how many?" Danni prodded.

"Six."

"I think I envy you. I always wanted a houseful of brothers and sisters."

He reached out a hand to help her up from her knees but made no effort to acknowledge her last remark.

"Why are you keeping the puppies here?" Danni asked, glancing around the enclosed porch. "I would have thought you'd put them in the barn."

Still holding on to her hand, Logan led her back into the living area of the cabin. "The new barn's not quite done yet. And with the old one being torched, I wouldn't feel right about putting Sassy and the pups out there."

"Torched?" Danni stopped, staring up at him in astonishment. "You mean it was deliberate? I thought it just . . . burned down."

"It did. With a little help." He pulled Danni's denim jacket off the wall peg and held it for her. "I'll show you around the rest of the place, if you like. Not that there's all that much to see, but I need to walk off Tucker's biscuits." He shrugged into his own flight jacket and again took her by the hand.

At the door, Danni turned back to Tucker, who was stoking the fire in the living room. "How long before I can take Chief home, Tucker?"

Tucker straightened, smiling. "No more than two or three weeks. I'll try to housebreak him for you in the meantime."

"Give that man a medal," she said, following Logan outside.

He draped one arm about her shoulder on the way to the barn. Danni knew it was just a casual gesture, but her feelings were anything but casual. She simply *reacted* to the man, almost in spite of herself. And it wasn't all physical, although she *was* attracted to him. Her response to Logan seemed to have much more to do with the *presence* of the man, the traits that made him what he was: the contrasts and contradictions, the quirks and the questions, the riddle, the puzzle, the enigma that made him . . . *Logan*.

"Why would anyone burn down your barn?" she asked him. They were now standing inside the new barn, Logan leaning comfortably against one of the stalls while Danni stooped to retie the laces of her tennis shoes.

"They got more than the barn," he said, his tone bitter. "About a year ago, Tucker and I bought a fine Charolais bull — a real prize. He was going to be the start of a small herd of quality beef cattle." His mouth turned down as he added, "The bull was trapped inside the barn with two heifers. We weren't able to save any of them."

"Oh, Logan — I'm sorry! How awful for you!"

A combination of hurt and anger crossed his features. "There wasn't anything we could do. It was late. We were both asleep. By the time we got out here, the barn was almost gone. Went up like a tinderbox."

"And you don't have any idea who would have done such a thing?"

He stared down at her, his expression hard. "Oh, I have an idea, all right," he said. "I just can't prove it. *Yet.*" After another moment, his mood seemed to lighten. "You cold, Half-pint?"

Danni nodded. "A little. I could use some more of Tucker's coffee."

"Sounds good," he agreed, pulling her to her feet, then holding her at arm's length as he searched her gaze.

They were close, very close, and Danni felt her heart begin to hammer at the look in his eyes. For one crazy moment she was certain he was about to kiss her, and she knew she wanted him to. But he didn't, and the moment passed, leaving her puzzled — and disappointed. Yet, in that moment of closeness, she had seen an array of emotions ricochet across his features and wondered if he had been as shaken as she.

They returned to the cabin to find a cozy

fire crackling in the fireplace and a fresh pot of coffee on the stove. Tucker brought out a pecan pie he had made earlier in the day, and the three of them sat around the table, eating pie, drinking coffee, and making idle conversation.

"I thought maybe your cousin Philip would be here this evening," Danni remarked.

"No, Phil never comes around. He's strictly a town guy. He thought I was crazy for buying a place way out here." Logan frowned. "Were you *hoping* he'd be here?"

Surprised at the sudden sharpness in his tone, Danni quickly shook her head. "No, of course not. I just thought since it's Thanksgiving, with your being family . . . you know. . . ." She let the sentence trail off, then moved to change the subject.

"Tucker, I can't decide which I like best — your biscuits or your pie. You're a wonderful cook!"

"Well, now, it surely is refreshing to hear a kind remark about my efforts in the kitchen for a change." Tucker darted a meaningful glance at Logan.

Danni, too, turned to Logan. "I hope you appreciate this man," she chided. "Why, Tucker is a better cook than my mother — and that's not small praise!"

"He's also going to be positively unbearable for the next ten days," Logan said, his mouth quirking.

"You're entitled, Tucker," Danni said, glancing about the rustic cabin with an admiring eye. "I really like your house," she said to Logan. "Was it here when you purchased the farm?"

He shook his head. "No, we put it up. Tucker did most of it. He's the craftsman. I just hammer nails and paint."

Danni stared with admiration at Tucker, sitting across from her, a quiet smile of pleasure on his face at Logan's compliment.

The entire cabin seemed to be a reflection of Logan's personality, Danni thought. The place was rustic, but not spartan, with a definite feeling of spaciousness. The living area and kitchen combined to form one large room with steps leading off the kitchen to a loft at the back of the cabin. The enclosed porch, where the dogs had been temporarily housed, served as Tucker's bedroom and sitting room. The walls were weathered siding, and the plank floors were bare except for two or three brightly colored rag rugs.

Logan mentioned that Tucker had made all the tables, which held a variety of salt-glazed jugs and baskets. Bookshelves lined one entire wall and among the books was what looked to be a state-of-the-art entertainment center. A large, rough-hewn mantel rested over the enormous stone fireplace, and above it hung a Confederate flag — no surprise there, Danni thought wryly. The windows were shuttered and without curtains. It was very much a man's sanctuary, yet it held a distinct warmth and charm.

Tucker collected their dishes, then excused himself to take a walk. Danni was surprised at his quick, deft movements, in spite of the fact that his entire right side from the hip down appeared to be quite stiff and almost immobile.

After a moment, Danni also pulled away from the table. "I should get going, Logan. I have to go in early tomorrow."

While Logan locked up in the back, Danni crossed the room to where a large, slightly scarred roll-top desk sat near the window. On top of the desk sat a framed photograph, and Danni picked it up for a closer look. Her heart wrenched at the sight of a younger Logan smiling out at her — a Logan with shorter hair and no beard, his arm around a tall, lovely young woman in a white suit. She was gazing up at the man beside her with an expression that clearly said he was her world. There was a happiness in Logan's face as well, a glow, an exuberance Danni had never seen.

Something akin to jealousy stabbed at her. At the same time Logan appeared at her side, and feeling suddenly guilty, Danni hurried to replace the photograph.

"That was our wedding picture," he said quietly.

"Your wife . . . Teresa . . . she was very beautiful."

He said nothing, but smiled a little, a smile that went to Danni's heart. She ached for the sadness she saw reflected in his face. Any envy she might have felt toward this woman who had made Logan so happy now fled.

They were both quiet for a long time on the way into town. Logan seemed content to drive in silence, and Danni couldn't shake off the troubling questions that had begun to plague her. Questions about what Logan was beginning to mean to her, and what, if anything, she might mean to him.

The night, thick with darkness and fog, echoed the silence of the car. Danni was startled when she felt his hand cover hers with a gentle squeeze. "I'm glad you came tonight," he said, glancing over at her. "Tucker really liked you."

"He's such a nice man, Logan. And he obviously dotes on you."

Logan continued to hold her hand as he slowed the car a little. "Tucker's a great guy." He paused, then added, "Actually, he's been a little like a father to me."

Danni was surprised by this rare frankness. "What about your real father? Is he still living?"

A muscle twitched in his jaw. "No," he said flatly. "Both my parents are dead."

"I'm sorry. I didn't know," she murmured. "What about the rest of your family? You said there were six of you?"

He didn't answer right away. When he finally spoke, his voice was unexpectedly harsh. "You must know about my family — you grew up here." Without giving her time to respond, he continued. "The last of the old-time sharecroppers. White trash, I believe we were called when I was a kid." He darted a glance in Danni's direction. "My father drank himself to death," he said, his tone flat. He expelled a long breath. "And I suppose my mother worked herself to death. Which makes for a brief family history."

Was the gruffness in his voice anger or embarrassment? Perhaps both, Danni decided. "I . . . suppose I was just enough younger than you that I wouldn't remember your folks," she said carefully.

He gave a strangled laugh. "It's not likely you'd have known them under any circumstances." Abruptly, he released her hand, then raked his fingers through the hair at the back of his collar.

"Logan —"

"I had four sisters and one brother," he went on in the same hard tone of voice. "My brother died in the state penitentiary a few years back. He was stabbed . . . during a riot. I don't see my sisters much. One took off when she was fifteen and never came back. The oldest, Julie, stays busy changing husbands. She's living in Scottsboro right now."

"And the other two?" Danni asked quietly, sensing his need to finish what he'd started.

"They're okay," he said a little more cheerfully. "Carrie — she's the youngest — went to college for a couple of years. She married a real nice guy. They live in Shreveport and have two little boys. Joanne isn't married. She's a nurse at a veterans' hospital in Georgia." His hands on the steering wheel relaxed slightly, but he continued to stare straight ahead of him as if no longer attuned to Danni's presence.

"I suppose all of us have some things about our families we'd just as soon forget, Logan."

He uttered a sound of disgust. "Danni, my *dog* has a better pedigree than I do, and that's no —"

A sudden hard thump against the car brought a scream from Danni. Logan swerved and hit the brake, but it was too late. A raccoon, its eyes reflecting the glare from the headlights, stared at them with wild eyes, then staggered and hauled itself across the pavement into the woods that ran alongside the road.

Logan stared after it. "Stay here. I'm going after it." Before the words were out of his mouth, he jumped from the Jeep and raced into the woods, leaving Danni to huddle alone in the cold darkness.

She knew when she saw him coming out of the thick grove of trees that he hadn't been able to find the raccoon. His walk was heavy, and there was a taut set to his features when he slid in behind the steering wheel.

He shook his head, saying nothing for a moment. He closed his eyes and leaned heavily against the seat. "I couldn't find him," he said. "He's either hurt bad and crawled off somewhere to die, or he wasn't hurt much at all and went on home to dinner."

"I'm sure he's all right," Danni reassured him. "It wasn't your fault, Logan. You couldn't have stopped in time."

"It *was* my fault," he said flatly. "If I'd had my eyes on the road where they belonged, it wouldn't have happened."

Danni watched him closely. "Don't be so hard on yourself," she said quietly. "You expect too much of yourself, Logan. You really do."

Still leaning heavily against the seat, he turned and looked at her. "Is there a charge for this counseling session, Half-pint, or is it on the house?" he questioned softly, his eyes lighting just a little.

Suddenly, inexplicably, Danni wanted to touch him — now, while his features were still unguarded and vulnerable. She did reach out her hand, halting just before her fingers would have brushed his face.

"You're a fake, Logan McGarey," she said softly, her voice thickened by a touch of surprise, as though she had just made an important discovery.

He looked at her, then covered her hand with his own much larger one, looking down at the fingers in his grasp as though he couldn't quite decide what to make of them.

With a slow, deliberate movement, he lifted her hand and placed it against the side of his face, holding it there, pressed gently against his bearded cheek.

"And what does that mean?" he questioned, an unsteady smile touching his lips.

Danni stared at her hand, marveling at the softness of the thick sable beard at her fingertips. Something in her throat swelled tightly, and she fought to keep her voice from crumbling. "You know exactly what I mean. You have everyone thinking you're such a tough guy."

His smile widened, became indulgent and just a little teasing. "Are you telling me I've blown my cover?"

Danni nodded, trying hard to swallow against the knot in her throat. Suddenly she could no longer bear the intensity of those midnight eyes. She turned to stare into the darkness all around them. "If you want to know what I think, I think you're about as hard-hearted as a lump of peanut butter."

"Is that right?" he asked quietly an instant before she heard the seat give with his weight. "Well, now, if you know me that well, then you also know I haven't entirely leveled with you about something else."

The question Danni had been about to ask died in her throat when she turned back to him. He had closed the distance between them, and there was something in his eyes that hadn't been there before . . . something soft and tender and infinitely caring.

His gaze never left hers as he slowly lowered her hand from his face to his shoulder, then gathered her into the warm circle of his arms. He was still smiling, his lips now just a breath away from Danni's. "I've been trying to convince myself . . . and maybe you as well . . ." he whispered, "that you're nothing more than a thorn in my side." His last few words were almost lost as he murmured against the side of her mouth. "But the truth is, sweet Danni, that you've become a lot more like an ache in my heart."

And then he kissed her, and suddenly it didn't seem to be night anymore. There wasn't any darkness outside the car or in . . . only the faint light in Logan's eyes and the warm, steady glow reaching out from her heart to his. Danni had never been kissed that way before, not by anyone. There was a sweetness in Logan's embrace, the touch of his lips on hers, that made her feel special . . . cherished . . . like the most precious gift in the world. She was sure he could hear her heart hammering. In her ears, at least, it sounded as if it were going to explode any moment.

When he finally moved his hands to her shoulders to put her gently away from him, Danni thought she saw reluctance in his face. She knew she saw a glint of surprise.

She could feel his hands trembling on her shoulders, and she searched his eyes, looking for something that might help her understand his feelings. But the intensity of emotion she encountered there almost made her draw away.

"What are you doing to my life, Half-pint?" he asked softly, his gaze burning into hers. "I haven't been right since I first saw you standing in a puddle at Ferguson's, looking like a sad-eyed kitten just washed up on the creekbank."

"You do have a way with words, Logan," Danni murmured, scarcely breathing as he very gently tucked a strand of hair behind her ear.

His smile was tender but uncertain. "Danni . . . I told you about my family because I wanted you to hear it from me. I need you to know exactly where I come from, what I am." His expression sobered even more. "I don't want any secrets between us."

Danni felt a wave of guilt wash over her. Did he know she was hiding something from him? As much as she hated this evasion, for now at least she had to keep her secrets. Unable to meet his probing gaze, she turned her face away. "You don't have to tell me anything you don't want me to know about your family, Logan," she said in a small voice.

With one finger, he lifted her chin and turned her toward him. "When a man is dead set on making a perfect fool of himself over a woman, the least he can do is be honest, don't you think?"

Wide-eyed, Danni stared at him, unable to halt the sudden riot of her feelings, instead going numb at the sweetness of his smile, the gentle warmth in his eyes. "I — I don't understand."

He kissed her lightly on the cheek just once. "Ah, Danni, you will . . . believe me, you will." His finger touched her cheek where he had kissed her, and his smile slowly faded as his eyes searched hers. "I don't suppose you'd allow me to lock you up in one of my cells for safekeeping, would you?"

"What — ?"

His expression grew even more serious as his fingers combed gently through her hair. "You worry me," he murmured, his eyes piercing hers as if trying to read her thoughts. "There's something — elusive —

about you. I can't shake the feeling that you may disappear into the fog one of these nights unless I hold on to you."

Suddenly, almost fiercely, he pulled Danni back into his arms. His large hand coaxed her head against his chest, his words nearly lost as he pressed his lips against her hair. "What am I afraid of, Danni? Why do I think I have to hold on real tight so you won't slip away from me?"

Not answering, Danni shut her eyes tightly and gave herself up, just for the moment, to his strength, the warm haven of his arms.

Oh, Logan. I hope you mean that. . . . I hope you will hold on tight because I don't want to slip away from you. . . . I don't want to lose you. . . .

The thought was scarcely out of her mind before a question replaced it, a question Danni had not until this moment dared to ask herself: what would it mean, when Logan finally learned the truth about *her?*

What would her deception mean to a man so intent on allowing no secrets to come between them?

Twelve

One week later, Danni was still wondering how many karate sessions it would take before she no longer felt like the victim of a mugging after each one. Granted, last night had been only her second class, but she had exercised fiercely during the week between the first two sessions, hoping to alleviate at least some of the pain.

So much for that theory, she thought, standing at her office window and giving a deep — but careful — stretch.

As she stood staring out at the overcast December day, she felt a lingering glow from the few minutes spent with Logan after class the night before. They had been together every evening since Thanksgiving, even when his work schedule allowed only a brief hour or two. He had walked her to her car after last night's class, on the way informing her that he had the coming weekend free and would like to take her to Huntsville for dinner on Saturday evening.

"We need some unhurried time to talk," he'd said before brushing a light kiss over her forehead.

Danni caught herself still smiling with anticipation, wondering at his cryptic words. But the nagging reminder that Logan's interest would surely flag once he learned that she hadn't been entirely honest with him quickly put an end to her lightheartedness.

A glimpse of movement at the infirmary roused her from her thoughts. Moving closer to the window, she saw Dr. Sutherland and one of the orderlies exit the building. Two elderly women walked between them.

The doctor was a member of the Colony who lived on the grounds. To Danni's knowledge, he never left the premises, at least during the day. He was one of those men who, for no identifiable reason, gave Danni the creeps. Young, plump, and smooth-skinned, he appeared harmless enough. But Danni had seen something in the hazel eyes behind the pop-bottle glasses that made her skin crawl. It was an expression — or lack of expression — that never failed to remind her of the photos she had seen of various concentration camp commandants.

She followed the quartet's advance up the walk to the main building, puzzled and somewhat disturbed by the strange parade. The scene was familiar, and she knew why. The women were walking with that same lifeless, undirected shuffle that had characterized the two men she had seen a few nights before. Sutherland and the orderly appeared to be escorting them, but something in the women's posture and gait made Danni suspicious.

There was something not quite right about that infirmary. It was nothing Danni could pinpoint, but her reporter's instincts told her that whatever was going on with these elderly "guests" was questionable, at the very least. She knew she should make Logan aware of her suspicions. But he was so obsessed with finding out what the Colony was up to that she feared he might come barging in and making accusations, or even arrests, thereby destroying her hopes of getting the entire story.

Which was reason enough to start pushing a little harder to *get* the story. Get the story and get *out*. Maybe she could also help Logan in the process.

She decided it was time to take a tour of the infirmary. Probably she could have been a little more creative, but as it was, the simple excuse of a headache worked well enough.

"I usually keep some aspirin in my purse or in my desk," she told the orderly at the infirmary in a little-girl voice that made her want to gag. She even stooped so low as to affect a drawl she had lost years ago.

The orderly was big and burly, and Danni had speculated upon occasion that he might be a little slow upstairs. But to his credit, he was eager to help when he saw her distress. He wasted no time helping her to a vinyl-covered chair and providing her with two aspirin and a cup of water.

Now he stood, arms crossed over his massive chest, beaming at Danni as though he might have just discovered the cure for the common cold.

Danni rewarded him with a wan smile. "I really do appreciate this. I'd never make it through the afternoon otherwise."

"Why don't you lie down for a while? Plenty of empty beds," he said with a magnanimous gesture.

"Oh — that sounds wonderful! But would it be all right?"

" 'Course it would. That's what we're here for."

I wonder, Danni thought. "Well . . . if you're sure, I think I'll just do that. But only for a minute."

She stretched out on the spotless, narrow bed, tugging the blanket over her as she feigned a weariness she didn't feel. While the orderly stood at the sink with his back to her, emptying and refilling an assortment of tubes and bottles, Danni quietly took mental pictures of the room, hoping to assimilate as much detail as she could. It appeared to be perfectly ordinary, antiseptically clean and furnished with only the necessities. There were several storage cabinets, a large sink, two examining tables, half a dozen empty beds, a small desk, and a hi-tech computer system.

The orderly turned just then and started toward her. Danni closed her eyes and pretended to be dozing. After another moment, she heard the door to the waiting room close, then the sound of the outside door being shut. Still she waited, lying very still.

Finally she opened her eyes, and, flinging off the blanket, went to the waiting room to look outside. She was relieved to see the orderly heading toward the main building, but she couldn't afford to delay. People came in and out of the infirmary all the time, so she would have to act as quickly as possible.

She wasted no time in going to the computer table and booting up the system. While she waited, she picked up a prescription pad lying on the desk nearby. A number of forms seemed to have been filled out and left for the signature of the staff physician. She flipped through the pad, making a quick mental note of some of the names: Cooper, Majors, Green, and others.

She turned the pad over to find a single name scrawled on the back. Slipping her glasses from on top of her head to the bridge of her nose, she studied the nearly illegible name — *Kendrick*.

William Kendrick again. The elderly "visitor" for whom Logan had been seeking information. She stared at the name another minute, then replaced the pad and went to the computer. The system was asking for a password. Danni scowled. She should have thought of that. She tried several obvious ones that got her nothing but a repeat of the "Access Denied" response. On a whim, she tried the numerical code for Reverend Ra's legal name, and she was in!

She had just opened a menu category for *Visitors* and found an alphabetized listing when a sound alerted her that there was someone outside. Danni glanced from the monitor to the door, furiously trying to think what to do.

It was going to take at least a few minutes to copy any files. She couldn't chance the orderly or someone else walking in on her. She made a lightning-fast decision to come back tonight, after curfew. She would be on the grounds late anyway, so she would just wait until everyone else had settled in for the night and try to find a way into the infirmary.

Swiftly, she shut the computer down and scurried across the room to grab her purse from the table by the bed. As she turned to leave, she spied a high, narrow window above the sink. An idea struck her, and again she crossed the room. Standing on tiptoe, she stretched up to release the inside lock on the window.

At the sound of voices in the waiting room, she froze for an instant. Then, taking in a deep, steadying breath, she squared her shoulders and whipped the strap of her purse over her arm. Faking a large yawn, she walked very slowly and deliberately into the waiting room.

The sight of Philip Rider standing near the outside door, deep in conversation with the orderly who had given her the aspirin, caught Danni completely off guard. For a moment she wondered if Rider shared Logan's resolve to drive the Colony out of Red Oak. Somehow she didn't think so. Although he was in uniform, his behavior toward the orderly appeared casual, even friendly.

Rider looked as surprised to see Danni as she was him, perhaps even more so. Still, his greeting was characteristically smooth as he removed his hat and nodded to her. "Miss St. John — Danni — I hope you're not ill."

For a moment Danni couldn't think what he was getting at. She recovered quickly, trying not to stammer her reply. "Oh — no. At least not now," she said. "I was just trying to get rid of a headache."

Rider regarded her with a look of concern. "Let's hope you're not coming down with the flu that's been going around. Nasty stuff."

"No, I'm fine," Danni insisted. "Really. I think I've just overdone it a little."

His look turned to something that made Danni uncomfortable. "I'm going to have to have a talk with Cousin Logan. He needs to get you home earlier at night."

Danni couldn't help but wonder if the remark wasn't calculated to indicate his awareness that she and Logan had been seeing each other. Not that it was any of his business. Still, she puzzled over his intention.

How did Philip Rider know about her and Logan? She somehow didn't think Logan would have discussed her with his cousin. She couldn't imagine Logan discussing his personal life with *anyone*. "Well, I really have to get back to work," she said, not meeting his gaze.

He caught her arm and accompanied her to the door. "I'll walk you back to your office. I've been wanting to see you anyway, but Logan keeps upstaging me."

What was it about Rider that put her on edge? He was always very polite, very pleasant. Very smooth. Too smooth, perhaps — was that what bothered her?

"Is there a problem?" she asked Rider as they started toward the *Standard* building.

"Problem?" He replaced his uniform hat at its former jaunty angle.

"Here at the Colony."

"Oh — no. Well, no more than usual," he corrected. "I'm just following up on some things Logan's been working on." He grinned down at her. "You probably know by now that he takes his job very seriously — especially when it involves the Colony."

Danni stole a glance at him, wondering if it was contempt she had heard in his voice, and, if so, the reason for it. She realized again that she simply didn't like the man. Even though Philip Rider was admittedly handsome, with a flirtatious self-assurance many women no doubt found attractive, he had the same effect on her as long fingernails being raked across a blackboard. A brief, tantalizing image of a darker man —

not quite so handsome, perhaps, but far more interesting — brought a sweet touch of gladness to her heart. The real problem was not Philip Rider at all, she admitted. And she had known that for some time now, hadn't she?

Her wandering attention returned when she realized that Rider had apparently asked her a question. "I'm sorry," Danni stammered.

She thought his smile might have been a little strained. "I asked how you like your job by now," he repeated.

"Oh, very much, thanks. It's been a challenge, but I'm enjoying it."

"Logan hasn't convinced you that you're living in sin, working for the Colony, then?"

Strangely angered by the question itself — and the unmistakable edge of sarcasm in his tone — Danni deliberately didn't reply. She was relieved when they reached the entrance to the *Standard* building.

Rider touched her arm lightly, offering an apologetic smile. "I'm sorry, I shouldn't have said that." Danni saw no real sincerity in his eyes as he went on. "I'm just concerned, Miss St. John — may I call you Danni? Logan sometimes carries his vendetta with the Colony too far. He means well, and I'm not saying he doesn't have reason to be suspicious." He frowned and looked out over the grounds of the Colony before continuing. "What worries me is that it seems to have become an obsession with him."

His expression was still sober when he turned back to Danni. "What I'm trying to say is that I hope you won't let Logan's feelings affect your job. You apparently like what you do, and it would seem to be a very . . . important position for someone as young as you." He flashed a winning smile and added, "You must have some dynamite credentials."

Danni stared at him, wondering what he was getting at. "I'm probably not as young as you think. I've had a lot of experience at what I do."

"I'm sure you have," he said, giving her a speculative look from his heavy-lidded eyes. "Incidentally, I would still like very much to take you to dinner. Is that ever going to happen?"

Danni was careful not to show her real feelings when she replied. "Not in the near future, I'm afraid. For the next few weeks, I'm probably going to be working most evenings."

"Well, I'm a patient man. I'll just keep trying until we can work it out." He touched his hat lightly, saying, "Have a nice evening now." Then he walked away.

Danni stared after him, noting that he returned to the infirmary rather than going to his patrol car.

Thirteen

It was always the same, Danni thought, slipping in between Add and Sister Lann later, perching on the floor with the others awaiting the entrance of Reverend Ra and his assistants. However, there was one difference tonight. At the last "Faith Service" she'd attended, she had seen only about a dozen elderly "visitors" among the students, including Otis Green, who had acknowledged her with only a blink of his owlish eyes. Tonight she was surprised to find three times that many. Where had they all come from in such a short time — and what exactly were they doing here?

As she had at the last service, Danni turned her attention from the scene around her for a moment and silently prayed that the Lord would forgive her for having even a small part in this. She found it difficult to endure these services, believing them to be a mockery of true faith. Still, she had never won a worthwhile exposé the easy way.

She found no problem in allowing Danni St. John to appear to be comfortably traditional, slightly helpless, and even a bit of an airhead. Indeed, it was a fairly easy role since, if she were to be brutally truthful about herself, she would have to admit that she *was* often hopelessly disorganized and unscheduled.

On the other hand, the heart of *D. Stuart James* burned with an unquenchable zeal to pull the plug on those unprincipled charlatans who preyed upon the helpless and made their fortunes by feeding on the lonely hearts of hurting people.

It was D. Stuart James who had worked six months as a ward secretary in a successful northeastern clinic. There, she had helped put behind bars the two physician-partners who had grown obscenely wealthy through a slick, nearly foolproof operation whereby healthy organs were obtained illegally, then sold via a blackmarket syndicate at astronomical prices.

It was D. Stuart James who had put her own life on the line by posing as the distraught wife of another freelance journalist — also a cancer patient. She had accompanied her "husband" to one of the most notorious healing centers for cancer in the world, where the two had eventually exposed the entire, fraudulent organization.

Now D. Stuart James was home and after the biggest story of her career, one especially dear to her heart. For D. Stuart James

— the pen name Danni St. John used for all her undercover journalism — hated, more than any other form of deception, religious fraud.

She had researched the Colony for months. Then, using the considerable credentials she had obtained under her real name, she'd managed to attain the position as editor of the *Peace Standard*.

So if sitting through one of Reverend Ra's phony Faith Services was a necessary evil, Danni resolved, sit through it she would. She knew full well that it might not be the worst of what she would experience before she got her story. And as she watched the young people all around her, bending over to touch their foreheads to the floor, chanting the usual meaningless nonsense, she wondered if that story might not be a great deal bigger than she had originally suspected.

She folded her hands and tried to appear interested while they repeated their Sacred Promise to the Master Guide. Reverend Ra — arms uplifted and eyes closed — now stood at their center as he softly voiced a number of affirmations to the prayers being sent up around him. He was an impressive sight, Danni had to admit. The white flowing robe and shining silver stole he donned for these services made the man a tall, shimmering spire in the midst of his followers.

As they began the communal chant, Danni shuddered. She kept her eyes closed and prayed fervently for the binding of any evil presence from the room. She especially disliked this particular part of the service, for she felt the chanting itself was a kind of hypnotic, mind-numbing experience for those involved.

Not that these young people needed anything else to deaden their brains, she thought bitterly. Without a doubt, Logan was right on target with his accusations about drug abuse. Danni wondered if anyone else, other than the leaders, was aware of the association of the Colony's complete name — Colony of the Lotus — with the drug culture.

The ancient Greeks had believed that the fruit of the lotus plant caused a dreamlike state, enabling one to escape reality. In the legends, the "Lotus Eaters" became so dependent on the plant and the resulting languor that they retreated farther and farther from the real world. Danni felt certain that this same phenomenon was happening to most of the members of the Colony, including her assistant, Add.

Although the youth now seated beside her often seemed torn and confused, occasionally he showed a spark of interest in Danni's faith or in a comment about God. Lately, however, Danni could almost see him slipping away into that misty, inaccessible place where the other students existed. The thought made her ill. With the soul of an artist and a highly gifted mind, the boy had such promise. If there were any way — any way at all — to get him out of this awful place, she intended to do just that!

When the service ended, Danni started to get to her feet, but Reverend Ra put out a restraining hand and asked everyone to wait. At that point, he called off a dozen or so names from a list handed to him by Brother Penn.

"Each of you has been assigned a city to visit. You will go out among the people who need to live again and bring them to us. Just as we have provided shelter for others in need" — he gestured toward the group of elderly men and women sitting to his left — "so will we offer a haven for all who would enter to find peace here with us."

Danni breathed a deep sigh of relief when Add's name was not among those called. "How do the students go about making contact with prospective guests?" she asked him as they filed out of the communal room.

"I've never been a guide," he said, waiting for her to exit the room ahead of him. "I've always worked within the family. But I think they go to the places where people in trouble can usually be found. You know — hospital charity wards, mission centers, bus stations. There are many who need us in those places."

"But why? I mean, why do it in the first place?"

He stared at Danni as if she were the adolescent and he the adult. "They need help," he replied simply.

"And they're willing to leave? To get in a van and come here with strangers?"

He shrugged. "We have much more to offer them than they already have. Why wouldn't they come?"

"What exactly *do* you offer, Add?"

He glanced around. Everyone was making their way to the dormitories, and Reverend Ra was talking with Dr. Sutherland. "You know," he said evasively. "Shelter, food, people who care — we meet their needs."

"How can the Colony afford to do that for so many?"

He gave Danni a blank look. "I don't know. It's all taken from the family bank, I suppose."

"The family bank?"

He nodded. "Whatever we have, we give to the family when we come here, and it's kept in trust for all of us."

"You mean you have no money of your own — none at all?"

His smile was puzzled. "Why would we need money? The Master Guide gives us everything we need."

Danni studied the finely sculpted young features, the glazed eyes. "Yes," she replied softly, "I'm sure he does."

She paused at the outside door. "I'm going back to the office for a while, Add. I'll see you tomorrow."

"Would you like me to go with you, Miss St. John?"

"No, no — I'm just going to tie up some loose ends and put some things away. It'll only take a few minutes." She waved as he disappeared around a corner.

The smooth voice at her back startled her, and she whirled around abruptly. "Well, Sister, it's good to see you among us tonight. I've been hoping you might show more interest in the family." Reverend Ra stood beaming down at Danni with what was supposed to be, she gathered, *fatherly approval.*

Danni slipped her glasses down from the

top of her head to her nose. "Yes. Well, it's been very . . . interesting. Different, of course. But interesting."

His smile appeared to be glued in place. "If you have questions about our philosophy or our work, Sister, please remember that I'm available to you at any time. I'll be only too happy to share and instruct you."

Danni felt almost as if he were physically drawing her into the depths of his sinister blue eyes. She had to steel herself against backing away from him as she mumbled, "Thank you. I'll . . . remember that."

"We haven't seen nearly enough of you, Sister. I hope we haven't placed too heavy a workload on those small shoulders of yours." He reached out a large, smooth hand to clasp Danni's shoulder.

Something in his gaze had changed. It struck Danni like a lightning bolt that the sanctimonious Reverend Ra was at the moment devouring her with his eyes — like a greedy man presented with a new menu.

Her mouth went suddenly dry. This time she did move away from him. "Not at all," she rasped, then cleared her throat and added, "I confess to being something of a workaholic. I enjoy being busy."

"Admirable," he said, removing his hand but not his gaze. "However, we want you to have time for spiritual growth as well. Please plan to join us more often."

Spiritual growth, indeed! Danni almost strangled, trying to stay silent.

"In fact —" his eyes flicked over her — "I had hoped we might have some time to get better acquainted — just the two of us. Since we share a common cause," he went on smoothly, "we really ought to know each other better, don't you agree?"

He moved in, his breath rancid in her face. "Let's have dinner tomorrow evening, shall we? Say, seven, in my quarters?"

His tone brooked no room for refusal. Danni desperately wanted to shout in protest at his retreating figure, but then it occurred to her that this might be an excellent chance to learn more about the esteemed *Reverend Ra*.

At ten-thirty, Danni left her office; hopefully no one would be wandering about the grounds at this time of night.

A cold dampness and heavy fog had settled in, giving the night air a clammy, oppressive stillness. Danni pressed herself against the end wall of the infirmary, listening but hearing nothing. Finally, she hoisted herself up on one of the trash barrels she'd tugged into place. With a quick look around, she began to slowly raise the window she had left unlocked. It didn't give easily; she had to brace one knee on the windowsill and push upward as hard as possible, almost losing her balance in the effort. But the last push did it. Quickly she swung over the sill and dropped lightly inside the dark examining room.

For one of the few times in her life, she was grateful for being a "half-pint," as her dad — and lately, Logan — had dubbed her.

Standing very still, scarcely breathing, she tried to decide whether she should leave the window open or close it. If someone happened by, an open window would be a dead giveaway. On the other hand, what if she had to get out in a hurry? She decided to take her chances with the open window.

The only light in the room was a dim glow from the outside security lamp a few feet away from the building, so she dug down into her skirt pocket for the small flashlight she'd brought along.

She tiptoed to the doorway of the waiting room, flashing a narrow beam of light in front of her. Satisfied that she was alone, she went back to the examining room and made her way to the computer.

With trembling fingers she turned on the system and waited for it to boot. The monitor illuminated the table enough that she switched off the flashlight and dropped it into her purse, then retrieved the diskette she'd brought with her.

Her hands were shaking so badly she could hardly get the disk into the drive. Quickly she typed in the password and was rewarded with a menu. Again she selected "Visitors," pressing the Enter key and watching an alphabetical list of names scroll down. She recognized some from the prescription pad. Beside each was some sort of number and letter that meant nothing to her.

Glancing at the open window, she reminded herself that she had to hurry. She could try to decode the symbols later. Hunched forward, she selected the Copy command, and the system began to download files onto the diskette. There appeared to be a hundred files or more, and she drew blood from her lower lip, biting it as she waited.

She jumped, then froze, at the sound of voices just outside the window. With her heart racing, she made her way to the window and peered out the side.

Two people engaged in conversation were passing by the infirmary. A closer look revealed that it was Brother Penn and an elderly man, his profile at first obscured. As a Hawk — the highest rank of students — Penn was allowed on the grounds later than those in the lesser ranks.

In the next instant, the two passed under the security light. The slight figure turned so that she had a clear view of his head in the dusky light. The ears were unmistakable. *Otis Green!* But where were they headed?

Holding her breath, Danni strained to hear the conversation, but couldn't make out what they were saying. Penn was speaking in a quiet, soothing tone to Otis Green, who seemed docile and agreeable to being led down the walk.

They didn't slow as they passed by, and Danni drew a quick breath of relief. Hurrying back to the computer, she released the diskette and turned off the system's power.

Her heart was still in her throat as she again edged her way to the side of the window. Looking in both directions, she crawled onto the barrel, forced the stubborn window closed, then jumped down and headed toward the parking lot. She didn't slow her pace until she was safely inside her car with the doors locked.

Thanks, Lord, she breathed, turning the key in the ignition. Relief draped itself around her like a soft, warm blanket as she pulled away from the Colony.

All the way home, until she was safely inside her own front door, she continued to murmur like a prayer one of her favorite verses from the Bible: "The Lord is on my side; I will not fear. . . ."

She had to see Logan. She had stayed up half the night printing out those files she thought might be important. But for the most part, she knew little more than when she started.

The documents marked *Kendrick* and *Jennings* contained the only information Danni could make sense of, and even that was limited. She had managed to figure out that each document was the equivalent of a personal file containing a variety of information about one of the deceased. A succession of dates seemed to indicate receipts and deposits of checks in a number of bank accounts. In addition, results of what appeared to be detailed investigations of each man were summarized with the conclusion that William Kendrick had no known living relatives who could be contacted. The other "visitor," on the other hand, had been a widower survived by a sister and two married daughters. A note to the effect that his current address at the Colony was being kept confidential upon his request had been entered into his file.

At two o'clock in the morning, Danni gave up trying to decode the mysterious symbols and numbers. Her brain was numb, and when she could finally keep her eyes open no longer, she admitted defeat and went to bed.

Her last thought before dropping off to sleep was that she would call Logan first thing when she got up and make arrangements to meet him and tell him about the files. Perhaps he would be able to help her make some sense of them. In doing so, of course, she would have to reveal the truth about herself. But she owed him that much. In fact, she was almost relieved that something had finally forced her hand.

Fourteen

Danni called Logan's farm at seven-thirty the next morning only to learn that he wasn't there.

Tucker sounded apologetic. "He left early. Had some kind of meeting in Huntsville. He said if you happened to call, I should tell you he'll be in touch as soon as he gets back."

"But you have no idea when that might be?" Danni pressed, frustrated that she wouldn't be able to talk to Logan immediately.

"It'll be late, I imagine." He paused. "Anything I can do?"

"No, thanks, Tucker. But if Logan should call, tell him . . ." Her voice trailed off. Tell him what? "Never mind. I have an . . . appointment . . . tonight anyway, so I won't be in until late myself."

She hung up, grabbed a glass of juice, and left the house.

All the way out to the Colony, Danni tried to shake off her somber mood. She was dreading her dinner "date" with the reverend tonight, dreading it even more than she would have expected. Only the possibility of learning something pertinent to the story made her determined to go through with the evening at all. Somehow, she promised herself, she would find a way to make it a very *brief* dinner. Even her determination to expose the cult might not be enough to enable her to tolerate its corrupt leader for an entire evening.

Danni worked late, right up to the time she was supposed to meet the Reverend Ra for dinner. She had been itching all day to get back to the infirmary computer, but she knew she dared not push her luck. Finally, with one eye on the wall clock, she straightened her desk and went to freshen up a little.

In the rest room, she studied her reflection in the mirror, not quite satisfied with what she saw. She had deliberately worn a plain navy suit to work, its severity unrelieved except for a white blouse. After another moment, she wiped away the last trace of lip gloss and, on impulse, twisted her hair into a tight bun at the back of her head, anchoring it with a rubber band. She shot a grim smile at her own reflection, deciding she now looked dull enough to cool any man's romantic ardor. Just in case the Reverend Ra was inclined in that direction.

As she took the deserted walkway with heavy steps, she prayed. She knew she probably should have her head examined for what she was about to do — and somehow she also knew Logan would be absolutely furious with her if he ever found out — but she was so utterly frustrated with her lack of progress on the story that she was almost desperate for a break. *Lord, I really need your help tonight, and your protection. There's something terribly wrong, something ugly, going on in this place. I have a part of the story, but not nearly enough to blow the whistle on this . . . unholy alliance. Not yet. Please, Lord, help me find what I need and keep me safe in the process. . . .*

By the time she approached the remote frame dwelling nestled in the midst of a dense copse of trees, Danni's heart was pounding with a vengeance. This was the darkest corner of the campus, and the dim trickle of light filtering through the miniblinds at the front windows did little to relieve the night shadows.

She raised her hand, but before she could knock, the door swung open. Danni sucked in her breath. The man standing before her bore little resemblance to the aloof cult leader with the correct air of reserve and professionalism he maintained during "business hours." Tonight Reverend Ra was not wearing his customary white suit, but a pair of khaki slacks with a casual shirt — blue — that warmed his cold eyes only a little; he also, Danni noted, had styled his hair in a more youthful, casual fashion. His appearance took Danni by surprise and left her groping to regain her composure.

"Come in, come in, Sister," Ra said, already ushering her inside. "I've been looking forward to this evening all day."

Danni walked woodenly into the room. Not only did Ra look like another person, here was another world as well — one of hedonistic splendor. The opulent furnishings — polished woods, rich fabrics, plush carpeting — spoke of great wealth and self-indulgent luxury. A fortune in art alone hung on the walls, and the surrealistic rendering of a scantily clad female figure made Danni quickly turn away, her face burning.

A large collection of candles in varying heights shimmered in reflection from gilded mirrors. At one side of the room, in an intimate alcove, a small table — its cloth the only touch of white in the entire room — was set for two. Bone china and sparkling silverware caught the glow of the candlelight. The dizzying scent of roses wafted to Danni's nose, and she coughed, desperately hoping she wouldn't have an asthma attack. Not here, with this man. *Please, Lord, not here. . . .*

Ra moved quickly to steady her. "Come, my dear, you've had a long day." He caught her arm, steering her to an enormous sofa, plump with cushions.

Without a thought, Danni sank down onto the sofa, almost immediately realizing she might have made a mistake. Something about the way her employer was regarding her made her want to leap and run.

Why had she ever agreed to come here to-night? And where was Logan when she needed him?

"Brother Sama!" Ra startled her by pressing a buzzer on the coffee table. A youth Danni recognized appeared almost instantly in the doorway, but he averted his gaze without acknowledging her. Instead he busied himself at the dinner table, pouring water, placing a salad beside each service plate. When he had finished, he stood back, head lowered, waiting for further instructions.

The boy appeared to be in a near stupor. Still, Danni wondered why he didn't at least look in her direction.

"Our sister is weak with hunger, no doubt." Ra turned his unwelcome attentions on Danni once more. "Yes, you do look rather pale, dear. I fear you've been working much too hard lately." With a sharp clap of his hands, Ra addressed the youth called *Sama*. "Serve the meal, and then you may be at your other duties."

In less than five minutes, Sama returned, this time wheeling a cart laden with silver serving dishes.

"Ah, splendid," Ra said, rubbing his hands together in anticipation. "That will be all, Brother Sama. You may go now. And be sure to lock the back door behind you when you leave."

The faint click of a key a moment later signaled that the young man had followed instructions. Danni again wondered at the power Ra apparently wielded over his followers. Or *was* it power? Could it be exactly what Logan suspected — some sort of drug abuse?

Or was it fear?

She suddenly realized that she was alone with a man she thoroughly disliked and distrusted. She jerked to her feet and pretended to inspect the room. "This is all so lovely," she said, moving from one ornate furnishing to another. "I would never have imagined anyone at the Colony living in such . . . style."

He seemed to interpret her words as a compliment. "Yes, it *is* nice, isn't it?" he said, beaming as he got to his feet. "I must admit that I look forward to my little retreat at the end of a busy day. It helps me to renew myself for . . . ministry." He paused, his eyes going over Danni in a way that made her skin crawl. "I invite very few people here, you know. *Very* few. Only those who are especially *important* to me — and to the Colony, of course."

"Well — I'm flattered," Danni managed to choke out. Then, trying for a touch of naiveté, she stopped in front of the table. "My, this all looks perfectly delicious. And I must admit I'm feeling a bit weak. I skipped lunch, you know, in anticipation of tonight."

The truth was she'd had no *appetite* for lunch, so tense had she been at the thought of the evening to come.

"Of course!" he cried. "Forgive me, my dear. I'm afraid my manners are somewhat rough. As I explained, I rarely entertain."

He pulled the chair out for her, his hands lingering on Danni's shoulders as she sat down. She suppressed a shudder, and after a moment he went to seat himself across from her.

"Ah! Perfect," he crooned, examining the

serving dishes. "Duck à l'orange, vegetables canned fresh from our own garden, and a choice of wine. What more could we ask?"

As he spoke, he removed a slender bottle from a bucket of ice, then popped the cork and passed it beneath his nose. "Splendid," he murmured, leaning across the table as if to fill the crystal tumbler at Danni's place. She made the observation that the restrictions regarding alcohol apparently didn't apply to the *Master Guide.*

Quickly, she covered the glass with her hand, shaking her head. "Water is fine, thank you."

He looked slightly miffed, but the smile remained fixed as he filled his own glass and returned the bottle to the ice bucket.

He stood to serve them, then again settled into the chair opposite Danni. Seeing that he had no intention of offering a blessing, Danni gave a silent prayer of thanks — adding another quick plea for protection — before forcing down a few bites of salad. She nearly recoiled on the taste of the duck — she *detested* this particular "delicacy" — and couldn't seem to get enough water. A fleeting, irrational thought of the scrumptious pizza she and Logan had shared not many nights past only served to curb her appetite even more.

What was she doing here? Why had she ever imagined she could go through with this?

Then she remembered why she had come and forced another bite of the despised duck down her throat. They ate in silence, Danni uncomfortably aware of Ra's scrutiny as she picked at her salad and pushed her vegetables around on her plate.

To make matters worse, an entire host of wild thoughts plagued her relentlessly throughout the meal. *What if she had given herself away somehow and Ra was suspicious? What if he had slipped something into her food, some sort of drug? Logan insisted there was a drug connection. No one knew she was here tonight. Not Logan or Tucker or — anyone. She should have told Logan the truth. What had she been thinking, keeping everything from him as if* she *were the criminal in all this?*

"So, tell me, are you enjoying your new venture with the Colony . . . Danni?"

Startled by his use of her name instead of the customary *Sister,* Danni fielded his question with one of her own. "Very much. But I'm curious about you, Reverend Ra. You've obviously won quite an impressive following. The Colony is growing, from all appearances. What brought you to a rural community like Red Oak?"

Preening under her apparent interest, Ra

launched into a lengthy recital of the Colony's history, carefully emphasizing his own preeminence. "When we outgrew the farm in Jonesboro," he rambled on, "we bought the Gunderson land. But that's a matter of public record. I should think a bright young journalist like yourself would know all about that. And that reminds me —" he leaned forward — "I liked your piece about our agricultural experiments — harvesting crops that are used to feed our own, with the surplus used for the underprivileged in town." He smiled widely, and Danni tried not to stare at his discolored teeth. "That's the kind of press we're after — lets the community know we're true servants — giving to the less fortunate, that sort of thing. That's what it's all about, isn't it?"

Danni decided to take advantage of his expansive mood. "I'm glad you were pleased. It's an admirable thing to care for those who can't take care of themselves — the destitute, the homeless. . . ." Hating herself, she pressed on. "I'm particularly interested in the elderly guests who visit the Colony. Are they part of some special project or benevolence?"

Ra steepled his fingers, regarding her through a haze of cigar smoke. He had pulled out a fat Havana after dessert. Another "exemption" from Colony rules, Danni noted. "They are the truly unfortunate — those with no kin and no means of support. They're safe and happy here —" he gave a sweeping gesture of his hand — "content to live out their days surrounded by people who care, rather than as nonentities, tossed out like useless rubbish into the streets."

Danni considered his carefully worded response. There was nothing new in anything he had told her. But what was he *not* telling her? She decided to risk one more question. "Are most of the elderly residents . . . ill . . . when they arrive?"

"Ill?" Ra seemed immediately on guard. "What do you mean?"

"Oh — nothing. I just thought with their age . . ." Certain she was treading on dangerous ground now, Danni moved to change the subject. "I hear the Colony is planning to sell produce at the Farmers' Market in Red Oak at reduced prices next year, in order to benefit the community. Why don't you give me some specifics for a follow-up article?"

Ra stubbed out his cigar in his coffee cup and pushed away from the table, his gaze devouring Danni as if she were an after-dinner mint. "The only follow-up I'm interested in right now is getting better acquainted with my newest employee."

Trouble. She might have known. . . .

Danni was not entirely inexperienced in matters of sexual harassment. She had even been stalked once by a fellow journalist — a photographer — who refused to believe she didn't find him irresistible. But the florid-faced Ra had the eyes of a predator and, based on her research, the morals of an alley cat. She knew instinctively that she dared not underestimate the man.

Determined to keep as much distance as possible between them, she met his gaze straight on. "What would you like to know first?" she said, biting down on self-disgust. At least, she reminded herself, she hadn't fluttered her eyelashes.

He leaned toward her, reaching for her hand. His breathing, Danni noted with revulsion, was decidedly heavy.

She could have slid off the chair with relief when the telephone shrilled.

Ra scowled but got to his feet. "I'll only be a moment."

Fortunately, the call took much longer. When he returned, Danni had already tugged on her coat and slung her purse over her shoulder. She made what she hoped was a coherent excuse about "really needing to get some rest," thanked him politely for the wonderful dinner, and beat a hasty retreat out the door.

Outside, she breathed a long sigh of relief as she half ran to her car. She was as frustrated and tense as she had ever been in her life, feeling that the entire evening had been a terrible waste. She had learned nothing, had accomplished nothing except perhaps to put the cagey Ra on alert.

Still, she *had* gotten a fairly revealing look at the persona Ra kept from his followers. And although it had been an unsettling experience, to say the least, her research — and her instincts — about the man had been confirmed.

She realized that Logan might find the information interesting. Just as quickly, she realized just how loath she was to have him know where she had been tonight.

Fifteen

By the next morning, Danni had still heard nothing from Logan. She went downstairs feeling out of sorts and exhausted. She had slept little, angry and humiliated that she had wasted an entire evening in a futile attempt to gain information from a man who was, she was now convinced, utterly corrupt.

She padded to the front door in her oldest bathrobe and stocking feet to bring the newspaper in, then went to turn on the coffee maker. While she waited for the Braun to work its magic, she unrolled the *County Herald* to browse the headlines.

Her heart lurched, her pulse hammering in her ears as she saw the screaming headline that capped a two-column-plus spread: *"SHERIFF ACCUSED OF EXCESSIVE FORCE AND BRUTALITY."*

A terrible sickness rose up in Danni as she scanned the article, the essence of which was that one of the Colony members — Brother Penn — and an elderly guest of the facility, "a gentleman named Otis Green" — had been detained at the county jail two evenings before, "allegedly for routine questioning."

The article went on, describing in detail Penn's charges that Sheriff Logan McGarey verbally harassed and humiliated the two of them, then proceeded to physically assault Penn, using "dangerous martial arts as a means of intimidation." Supposedly, Penn had displayed a number of bruises and lacerations to reporters, injuries which he claimed were a result of "the sheriff's terrorizing tactics."

Almost as bad as the screaming headline was the sly, unnecessary reference to Logan's family. The fact that his brother had died in prison during a riot was a prominent part of the article, coupled with a comment about one of his sisters disappearing during the time Logan was "earning medals for valor in the Desert Storm conflict." This was yellow journalism at its worst, and Danni was outraged. What made it even more painful was the memory of the hurt she had sensed in Logan the night he told her about his family. Somehow she sensed that this article would be like pouring salt in an open wound.

Hurling the paper to the floor, she tore out of the kitchen and raced upstairs to change. By the time she jumped behind the wheel of her car, she was livid. The entire story was a lie!

She had seen both Penn and Otis late on the night the beating supposedly took place, the same night she had sneaked into the infirmary. It had been dark, of course, but she had seen both of them clearly enough under the security light. That had been well past ten-thirty, and she was certain Penn had had no bruises or cuts of any kind. Besides, she knew Logan well enough to know he would never abuse his karate skills in such a way. This was a deliberate attempt to discredit him.

It didn't take a rocket scientist to figure out what *someone* — whoever had ordered Penn and Green to stage their little charade — hoped to accomplish. The election was only weeks away, and Logan was a definite threat to the Colony. Danni couldn't quite figure out how Ra was involved, but he *was* involved, all right, and she was sure of it. The Colony — and Ra — would eliminate their major adversary by getting Logan out of office.

Well, they weren't going to get away with it! Danni fumed, driving too fast, gripping the wheel until her hands ached as she went over the article in her mind. The paper said that Penn and Green had been released at nine-thirty, over an hour before she had seen them.

Then it struck her. She couldn't prove anything of the kind, not without divulging her own whereabouts that night. She couldn't very well reveal the fact that she had broken into the infirmary in an effort to download files off the Colony's computer!

The reality of her dilemma hit her like a blow. In order to clear Logan, she would possibly have to incriminate herself in an illegal activity — and in the process blow her cover. That would mean the loss of months of research, as well as the loss of a story she considered of monumental importance — perhaps of even more importance than she had originally suspected. If her instincts were right, there were atrocities taking place at the Colony that no one would have imagined — atrocities involving the elderly "visitors" being housed in increasing numbers. Somehow, she *had* to get this story. The truth might actually save lives, not to mention the *souls* of dozens of young people trapped behind those walls.

But if her silence would endanger Logan, how could she *not* tell the authorities what she had seen that night? Irreparable harm might be done to him. His integrity would be suspect. The election might well be lost. Criminal charges might even be brought against him! There was no way she could stand by and let that happen.

Aside from her personal feelings for him, Danni was convinced that Logan was a good sheriff, that he might in fact be the last, best hope for the entire town of Red Oak. No one else seemed to have a clue as to what was going on at the Colony. The community *needed* Logan as sheriff.

In that instant, she made the decision to tell Logan everything she knew. And if it took her own involvement to clear his name, then she would also go to the authorities. If the truth would save him, then he would have that truth today.

Danni stuck her head inside the doorway of the office waiting room, but saw no one. When she entered, she could hear Logan talking in another room; after a moment she decided he must be on the phone. She sat down on an uncomfortable wooden chair and picked up a magazine. Seeing that it was over a year old, she leafed through it distractedly, then tossed it aside. The minute she could no longer hear Logan's voice, she got up and went to the door.

At her approach, he quickly pushed away from his desk and came around to greet her. Something tugged at Danni's heart when she saw the shadows under his dark eyes.

His uniform, at any other time immaculate and perfectly pressed, was rumpled. He looked tired, almost haggard, and suddenly older. But his smile was warm with apparent pleasure at the sight of her.

She walked the rest of the way into the office, not quite knowing what to say. "I saw the paper," she finally blurted out.

He nodded, searching her eyes. "You and everyone else in town."

"They can't get away with it." When he didn't answer, she pressed, "Can they?"

His shoulders sagged for only an instant before he straightened and closed the distance between them. "Then you don't believe it?" he asked quietly. The relief in his tone was unmistakable as he took both her hands in his.

Danni almost lost her breath when she encountered the depth of emotion in his eyes. "Of course, I don't believe it, Logan! Even if I hadn't —" She stopped. This wasn't the place for what she had to say to him.

"If you hadn't *what?*" he prompted, frowning.

"Logan, there's so much I have to tell you! We need to talk."

He started to lead her to the chair in front of his desk, but Danni hesitated. "Not here," she said, clasping his arm. "I —"

The sound of the outside door slamming shut stopped her, and she released Logan's arm. Philip Rider's mildly taunting voice reached them before he appeared in the open doorway. "Well, Cuz, you've done it this time! I told you that temper of yours was going to —" He broke off, his eyes going from Logan to Danni as a slow, mocking smile broke over his features. "Sorry," he drawled with exaggerated emphasis. "I'll come back —"

"That won't be necessary," Danni said firmly before he could finish. "I was just leaving." She held Logan's gaze for only a moment. "I'll . . . see you later this evening, then? For dinner?"

He studied her, then nodded. "Right. About seven?"

"Fine. Nice seeing you again, Deputy Rider," Danni said briskly, not looking at him as she left the office, head high.

She imagined that she could feel his insolent gaze on her until she was out of sight.

Sixteen

Danni left the Colony early that afternoon. By the time Logan arrived, she had made an extra printout of all the files on the disk so she could give him a copy. She had just managed to shower and change when he arrived, early.

Still in uniform, he removed his jacket and gun, leaving them in the closet, before coming the rest of the way into the hall. "Sorry I didn't have time to change," he said. He came to her then, drawing her into a quick embrace and kissing her lightly, as naturally as if he did it every day.

"So what's going on?" he said, holding her at arm's length, studying her.

Flustered by his closeness — and tense to the point of despair — Danni started to pull away from him. "Dinner first," she said. "I knew you'd be tired, so I thought we'd eat here."

He caught her arm, drawing her back to him. His dark eyes went over her face, and he gave her a tired smile. "You don't want to be seen in public with the strong arm of the law, is that it?"

"Logan —"

"Just . . . let me hold you for a minute. Please?"

His quiet appeal enfolded Danni like a sweet caress. She rested her head against his heart, standing quietly in his arms. If it occurred that he might not be so eager to touch her after tonight, she quickly dismissed the thought, instead drawing strength from his closeness.

When he finally released her, she led the way into the kitchen. "What kind of reaction have you had from the article so far?" she asked him.

His characteristic grin looked a little forced. "Oh, about what you might expect. I'm not too popular at the moment." He watched her go to the refrigerator. "You really don't have to feed me, you know. I'm not all that hungry."

"Well, I am," Danni fibbed. "There's ham and roast beef, if you don't mind cold cuts."

"I don't suppose you have any buttermilk?"

"As a matter of fact, I do," Danni informed him smugly.

His dark brows shot up in surprise. "I think I'm in love," he said.

Danni knew he was joking, but her heart suddenly tumbled over itself. She cleared her throat. "Tell me what this is all about," she said, taking what she needed from the refrigerator.

Logan rolled up his shirt-sleeves and started to slice off some roast beef while Danni fixed a platter of ham and cheese. "Night before last, I went over to the bus station to pick up a package that was due in from Chattanooga," he said, wielding the knife like a machete. "Penn and this fellow, Green, were standing at the ticket counter." He put the knife in the sink and carried the plate of roast beef over to the table. "What else do you want me to do?"

"That's all. Sit down, and we'll eat."

He held Danni's chair for her, then scooted in close beside her, waiting while she offered a prayer of thanks.

"So — go on," Danni prompted as they filled their plates.

"Well, they were arguing," he explained, spearing a pickle. "Green — the old fellow — seemed upset. I started asking him some questions, and he said he just wanted to leave, but Penn wouldn't let him go. He said the old man was sick and didn't have any business leaving the Colony. Green grabbed on to me and started mumbling something about them keeping him a prisoner. He seemed scared. At that point, I put them both in the patrol car and took them downtown for further questioning."

"Then you didn't actually arrest them?"

"I never even mentioned the *word 'arrest'!* I thought maybe Green needed help — I noticed he couldn't get in the patrol car fast enough. Penn sulked all the way downtown, but he's always a little strange, I didn't pay much attention to him. The old fellow, Green — well, he was obviously stoned on something. Agitated one minute, out on his feet the next."

Danni frowned. "Mr. Green seems like such a nice little man. But I've wondered about him, lately . . . he hasn't acted like himself. So you let them go? You didn't detain them at all?"

Logan muttered a short sound of disgust as he helped himself to another glass of buttermilk. "We hadn't been in my office half an hour before the old guy did a complete about-face. Started making noises about being sick, and insisting that Penn was only trying to help him." He paused. "That started *after* I went down the hall to get him some coffee, thinking to clear his head. By the time I got back, Green was claiming that the whole thing was a mistake, that he just wanted to go back to the Colony with 'Brother Penn.' " He shrugged. "So, yes, I let them go."

Danni thought for a moment. "Wasn't there anyone else in the office at the time?"

Logan shook his head. "Phil had been there, but he took a call out on Brumleigh Road and didn't get back in town until later. No, there was no one around but me. Unfortunately," he added, his expression grim.

Troubled, Danni left the rest of her cold supper untouched. "Why would Otis Green suddenly change his story like that? And why in the world would he charge you with brutality, when you were only trying to help him?"

Again Logan shrugged. "It was a setup. I should have seen it coming."

Danni watched him, wondering how he could be so seemingly matter-of-fact about something so potentially destructive. "Do you really believe that?" she asked quietly. "That this was all a deliberate attempt to make trouble for you?"

He looked at her. "Don't you?" he countered.

Danni put her hands to her temples and pressed against the pain that had begun to drum its way up her skull. "I don't know what to think," she said dully.

With a scowl, he leaned back in the chair. "Not that I haven't thought about knocking a few heads out there at the Funny Farm."

Danni shot him a look, and he grinned at her. "I said *thought* about it, honey. I'm not that stupid."

The endearment that had escaped him so easily caught Danni off guard. But then Logan had a way of surprising her when she least expected it.

She rose and began clearing the table. "What are you going to do?"

"There's not much I *can* do," he replied, getting up to help her. "The fact is that Penn is walking around with some ugly bruises and cuts on his face, and as long as Green backs him up, it's my word against theirs."

Danni stopped, her back to him. "Maybe not," she said softly.

"What?" He had gone to the refrigerator to replace the trays of meat, and seemed to be inspecting the contents for something else.

"I said," Danni repeated, taking their plates to the sink and turning to face him, "that it's *not* just your word against theirs."

She had his attention now. He ducked his head out of the refrigerator and closed the door. "What does that mean?"

Her hands shook as she poured a mug of coffee for him, then one for herself.

"Danni?"

"Let's go into the living room," she said, handing him his coffee.

Logan took the mug of coffee from her, still searching her face, then reached to take Danni's cup as well.

"Why don't you make a fire?" she said as they entered the living room. "I need to get something."

When she returned from the den with the printouts, she placed them on the coffee table and sat down on the sofa.

The fire caught, and Logan came to sit beside her. "What's this?" he asked, glancing at the file folders.

"I'll explain." But for a moment Danni sat staring into the fire, groping for the right words. What she was about to tell him should help to clear him of the false charges. But it might also turn him completely against her, and the thought was almost more than she could bear.

And yet, she really had no choice. "Logan," she said, turning to face him, "I meant what I said in the kitchen. I think I can prove that you didn't touch Penn or Otis Green."

He frowned and set his coffee on the table. "What are you talking about?"

Danni pulled in a ragged breath. "I saw them — both of them — that same night, long after they would have left your office." She swallowed against the dryness of her mouth. "I can vouch for the fact that there wasn't a mark on Penn."

He shook his head, his frown deepening. "I don't understand. Where were you?"

"Inside the infirmary," Danni replied, averting her gaze. "I saw Penn and Otis Green from the window. They passed directly under the light."

"What were you doing in the infirmary at night? What time was this?"

"Probably close to eleven."

Her reply brought a look of something akin to relief, or hope, to his features, only to be almost instantly replaced by one of confusion. "What were you doing out there so late?"

"I told you, I was in the infirmary."

"You haven't told me why."

Danni could no longer meet his dark, questioning gaze. "I was . . . copying some files off the computer's hard drive," she said, looking into the fire.

"Copying —"

Without looking at him, Danni gestured with one hand that he should hear her out. "I hadn't been inside very long when I heard voices. I looked out and saw Penn and Mr. Green. I couldn't hear their conversation, but I could see them. And Penn looked perfectly fine to me," she said, her tone hard as she finally turned back to face Logan. "No cuts. No bruises."

His face was a study in bewilderment. "I seem to be missing something here. Did you happen to mention *why* you were copying files off the Colony's computer? And how did you get in anyway? They lock up every building on the grounds like a vault before sundown." He stopped. "What's this all about, Danni? Talk to me."

Danni reached for one of the folders on the table in front of them. "I made a printout of some of the files I copied. I can't make much out of this, but maybe you can." She handed him the folder, then rose from the sofa and went to stand in front of the fire, watching him.

"Does any of that make sense to you?" she asked after a moment.

Intent on the page in front of him, he gave a slow nod. "This is some sort of personal file on William Kendrick, apparently. There's a record of bank deposits and —" He broke off, tracing down the page with one finger, then glancing up at Danni. "Same amount each month. Deposited in different banks. That would seem to indicate some kind of a pension or government check, don't you think?"

Danni shrugged. "There are others similar to that one. One is for someone named Jennings."

Logan dragged his gaze away from Danni and went to the next folder.

"Jennings was the first 'guest' to die at the Colony," he murmured as he leafed through the file folder. "At least, the first I'm aware of."

He reached for another folder, and Danni said, "That's just like the others. Another listing of bank accounts and some odd numbers and symbols I can't make out."

Logan went on scanning the files, one after another, saying nothing. Occasionally he gave a soft whistle or a low sound of recognition. Finally he looked up. "These would seem to be logs," he said. "Laboratory journals of experiments."

Danni expelled a sharp breath. "What kind of experiments?"

Logan took his time stacking the folders neatly on the table. Then, slowly, he stood and came to stand directly in front of her. "Drug experiments would be my guess." His voice was rough, his dark gaze severe. "I think you'd better tell me everything. What are you doing with these files, Danni? What exactly is going on here?"

No longer the man she had come to think of as gentle and often vulnerable, he looked and sounded very much the sheriff now. Danni turned away. "This is going to take a while," she said. "You'd better sit down."

He caught her by the shoulders, turning her face to him. "Tell me," he demanded, his eyes sparking with anger. "Tell me the *truth*."

Seventeen

Logan was slow in releasing Danni. Even as he followed her back to the sofa, he kept one hand on her shoulder, as if to make certain she wouldn't slip away.

From the couch she leaned forward to retrieve a thin blue folder she had placed beneath the others. She emptied it, putting a couple of press cards aside as she handed Logan a sheaf of photocopied articles.

Glancing from her to the file's contents, he thumbed through the articles, scanning each quickly. "I've seen some of these," he said, still reading.

After another moment, he spread the articles out side-by-side on the coffee table and turned back to Danni. Mutely, she handed him the two press cards, one imprinted with the name *Danni St. John,* the other, *D. Stuart James*.

He looked at them, turned them over, then leaned forward to check the by-lines on the papers in front of him before again turning to Danni. "I give. What's all this?"

Danni tried to smile, failed, and sat watching as his glance again traveled from the press cards to the articles. He caught a sharp breath, and now Danni saw a glint of understanding begin to dawn.

"*You* wrote those?" he said, inclining his head toward the coffee table. "This is some sort of a pseudonym —" he held up one of the press cards — "this *D. Stuart James?*"

Danni nodded, her heart wrenching as she saw his eyes already clouding with doubt and suspicion. "It's just a name I use for . . . certain kinds of stories."

"Certain —" He blinked. "What *kind* of stories?"

Danni swallowed, avoiding his eyes. "Exposés, mostly."

His eyes narrowed as something seemed to click, and he pulled back a little. "Exposés," he said, his tone flat.

Again Danni gave a nod, still not looking at him. "I used it with my first piece of investigative reporting, and I decided to keep it. It's a combination of my mother's maiden name and my father's given name."

"I don't understand. What kind of stuff are you writing that you can't use your own name?"

Danni let out a long breath. "I do it to protect my family — my mother. I've dug up some fairly . . . controversial stories. I didn't want to take any chances."

She felt his eyes on her, looked at him,

and saw his confusion, his questions. But at least he didn't seem angry . . . yet.

He glanced at the articles, one of which dealt with the cancer clinic scam, another the exposé of the daycare center for the elderly. In one form or another, the other stories all dealt with some form of treachery — schemes that existed for the sole purpose of duping the innocent, whose needs often made them desperate, easy victims for the unscrupulous.

"This is heavy stuff," he finally said, regarding her with an expression Danni couldn't read. "Scary stuff. Why do you do it?"

Danni shrugged, again made the effort to smile. "Believe it or not, I do it because I think it's what I'm . . . called to do."

He said nothing, clearly waiting for more of an explanation. "Some people go to the mission field," Danni said haltingly. "Others become pastors or doctors or counselors. Me — all I've ever been good at is writing. And I've been really fortunate, making a good living at what I like to do." Danni paused, struggling for just the right words. She genuinely wanted him to understand why this was important to her. "But I wanted more than just a good living, don't you see? I wanted . . . to make a *difference*."

She attempted another self-conscious smile. "You know — for people. For the world. I wanted to do something for God, something that would last."

Logan searched her eyes for a long time before he finally gave a slow nod, saying, "Okay. I can understand that. But where does it fit in with what you're doing now? With the Colony and these files and —"

He stopped, his eyes flaring. "Oh, no. No, you're not that crazy."

"Logan —"

He jumped to his feet, stood glaring down at her. "So *that's* what this is all about! The job is just a front. You're after another *story!*"

"Will you just let me *explain* —"

He moved closer, his face a thundercloud. "You *are* crazy! Do you have any idea what you're mixed up with here?" He was almost shouting at her now as he towered over her.

"Yes!" Danni shot back. "I *do* know! That's why I'm here!"

Logan regarded her with a look of incredulous fury that made Danni want to shrink and hide. But she forced herself to face him, refusing to let him see that his tirade had brought her close to tears.

Somehow, she managed to keep her tone level, her voice tightly controlled. "It's my job, Logan. It's what I do."

"It's what you do," he echoed mockingly. "I don't suppose," he said, lowering his tone to a threatening hiss, "that it ever once occurred to you to just tell me the truth from the beginning? Have you enjoyed this little masquerade? What, it's a game for you, is that it? *Outwit Your Local Sheriff?*"

Danni snapped. The combination of sleepless nights, Logan's anger, and her own tension rushed in on her like a tempest. She leaped up from the couch, eyes blazing. *"Stop it!* Just — *stop it!"*

He actually stepped back, his surprise at her outburst obvious.

"Correct me if I'm wrong, *Sheriff,* but I'm reasonably sure it was you waxing eloquent just the other night about the dangers of indifference, the inherent evil of a do-nothing attitude. What was it you quoted? *'The only thing necessary for the triumph of evil is for good men to do nothing.'* Tell me, does that exclude women or just me?"

The muscle in Logan's jaw flexed, and the dark brows shot up. "You have a point, I assume?" His tone was infuriatingly calm.

"The *point,"* Danni bit out, "is that I'm only following your lead. I'm putting my proverbial money where my mouth is! But for some reason that seems to have set you on the warpath. Why is it that you expect everyone else but *me* to have the courage of their convictions?"

"Because I've already lost *one* woman I loved!" he rumbled, his face a dark mask of rage. "I'm *not* going to stand by and watch it happen all over again!" The minute the words exploded from him, the anger that had darkened his features only a moment before gave way to a look of stunned awareness.

They stared at each other — the veneer suddenly stripped away, the truth finally revealed, their defenses totally down. Within seconds, there was nothing left in Logan's eyes but the reality of his admission. Danni could do nothing but stand, unmoving. He took a step toward her. She backed away . . . but not too far.

"Danni?"

He stood looking down at her, his eyes filled to overflowing with something achingly familiar, yet somehow new. They were close, so close, and Logan caressed her with his eyes long before he gently tilted her chin to lift her face toward his.

The softness, the tenderness in his eyes were Danni's undoing. She tried to smile, a futile thing that quickly faded. "Well," she choked out. "I suppose that's as good a reason as any."

His arms came slowly around her, drawing her into the safe haven of his strength. Danni melted against him, and she felt his trembling blend with her own. And then he kissed her, so carefully, so gently, and with such reverence Danni felt certain she would never, ever feel quite so fragile or so cherished as she did at this moment.

She leaned her head on his chest, felt the hammering of his heart echo her own, heard his soft sigh. Her heart swelled with a strange new kind of happiness. They stayed locked in each other's arms for a long time, and Danni prayed that, no matter what happened in the future, she would be allowed this feeling, the memory of this moment, forever.

Finally, Logan brushed her temple with his cheek, pressed his lips to her forehead once, and whispered, "Ah, Danni . . . Danni, I do love you."

Danni felt her hopeful heart trip over itself. "Logan . . ." She stopped, but she could no longer keep the words bottled up inside her. "I love you, too. But . . . it's happened so quickly. . . ."

His smile deepened. "Not really," he said. "At least not for me. I knew your first night in town that I was a goner. The way you curled up under that old blanket in my office and glared at me for a solid hour —" he shook his head — "I knew right then that I was in serious trouble."

He continued to hold her for another moment. "What I said earlier — the way I flew at you —"

Danni tried to tell him she understood, that he had a right to be angry with her, but he silenced her, easing her back just enough that he could press a gentle finger to her lips. "No, let me say this. We haven't talked . . . about Teresa yet. And we need to. I want you to know what happened. What it was like for me."

He took her over to the sofa and pulled her down beside him, slipping an arm around her shoulders. "Teresa was the first woman I ever loved — the *only* woman, until you. She was the first person who ever loved *me*." A sad smile crept over his features, and he shook his head a little. "She made me feel like I was ten feet tall. We were really happy together, and it was the kind of happiness that would have *lasted,* you know?"

Danni nodded. Instead of the jealousy she might have expected to feel at his words, she knew only an overwhelming sense of sorrow for him, and for Teresa . . . and for all they had lost.

"She died in my arms," he went on, "in the middle of a shopping mall, surrounded by strangers."

He dropped his arm away now, leaning forward on the edge of the couch. When he continued, his voice was hoarse, as if anguish were wringing the very words from him. "I couldn't do anything for her . . . nothing but hold her . . . and watch her die." He shuddered. "May I never feel as helpless as I did that day. I wanted to die *with* her."

His shoulders slumped, and Danni moved to touch him. "Oh, Logan. I am so sorry! I can't even imagine what it must have been like for you."

He turned to look at her. "She was a teacher. She loved children. We planned to have a bunch of them . . . that's what we both wanted." He stopped, squeezed his eyes shut, but only for an instant. Suddenly, he caught Danni by the shoulders, clasping her tightly as his dark eyes drew her into his pain. "It was all taken away from her — everything she wanted. And from me. She never had a chance. But *you do,* Danni. That's what made me so angry. When I thought about you deliberately risking your life . . . to get a *story* . . . I just — snapped. You don't have to do that. I'm asking you *not* to do it!"

Sick with dismay, Danni could think of nothing to say, nothing that would help him understand.

His gaze burned into hers, no longer with anger, but with what appeared to be a desperate plea for her submission. "Promise me you won't go back to the Colony."

"Logan, I can't . . . I'm so close, don't you understand, I'm so *close!*"

"Listen to me!" His features contorted, an angry flush staining his skin. "*You're* the one who doesn't understand! I think someone knows about you, knows who you are, what you're doing here —"

At Danni's attempt to protest, he tightened his grasp on her shoulders almost painfully. "Your house has been ransacked — twice. You told me yourself you think someone was watching you, watching the house, the last time it happened. And these articles you've shown me —" he glanced toward the papers on the coffee table — "what if someone else has seen them?"

Danni hadn't even thought of that. She bit her lower lip, saying nothing, and he relaxed his grip on her a little. "Don't you see?" he said, lowering his voice. "You could be in real danger."

"There's no reason to think they'd actually *hurt* me, Logan, even if they were to somehow find out —"

"They have murdered three people, woman! Maybe more!" He was shouting again, and Danni shrank beneath the violence of his words.

"Murdered?" she echoed, her voice thin. "You can't know that. . . ."

He released her, whipping around and snatching up the printouts from the table, then shoving them at her. "I know it. And now I can *prove it!* With these. There's a record of drug experiments performed on two separate individuals here — both of whom died on the premises. There's a record on the third somewhere, you can take that to the bank. I'll have to study them in depth, but I already know what I'll find, based on the drugs that are mentioned in these records. Let me give you my best guess — and it's an educated one, by the way — Kendrick and Jennings died either from being deliberately overdosed, or because someone got careless."

Danni studied his face, the faint whiteness about his mouth, the rigid set of his features. "You can tell that much . . . just from those printouts?"

He nodded, tossing the papers back to the table. "It looks to me as if their own mad scientist — that's the wild-eyed Dr. Sutherland — has been overdosing some of the elderly 'guests,' probably just enough to make them cooperative, at first. Apparently, these people aren't entirely without funds. A number of checks — social security and welfare, I'd imagine — have been signed over to the Colony and deposited in different banks all over the state. But according to some of the entries in those files — Sutherland is identified as the writer, by the way — they've been experimenting with some real mind-benders. I'd need the rest of the log entries to prove it, but it looks to me as if those poor souls died from something other than natural causes."

"But you need proof?" Danni said thoughtfully, mulling over what he'd told her.

"And I'll get it." His tone left no room for doubt. "Somewhere in that infirmary, there's a record of the most recent experiments — and the results. I've got a hunch that Sutherland is just crazy enough to keep a record of *everything* — his failures as well as his successes, and who knows what else." He stopped, then added in a tone laced with resolve, "I'll get the proof. One way or another, I'll get it."

Danni's mind was racing. She was convinced Logan was right. But even if he were, there was no way he could get safely in and out of the infirmary. His very presence on the grounds would be interpreted as a threat, would put Ra and the others on alert. No, it would be entirely too dangerous.

But *she* could get what Logan needed. With a strangely calm detachment, Danni went on to think it through. No one would raise an eyebrow at her working overtime. She had already established a routine of doing just that. All she needed was one more trip to the infirmary. Just one. She could get the proof Logan needed — and the proof *she* needed, for the story. If Logan was right . . . and she believed he was . . . they could close the doors of the Colony and clear Logan's name in time to save the election for him.

"Whatever you're thinking, forget it." His warning broke through her thoughts. "I don't trust that look."

She smiled at him. "You read minds, too?"

"Don't I wish?" he muttered. "Danni, give me your word that you won't do anything stupid."

Danni caught her lower lip between her teeth and glanced away.

His hand on her arm made her turn back to him. "Promise me," he urged, frowning.

Danni hesitated only an instant. "I won't do anything stupid," she assured him, meaning it.

And she *wouldn't*. She would be careful, extremely careful, in light of what she had learned tonight. But all the same, she would do what she had to do, for the story . . . but mostly for Logan.

She no longer felt that she had a choice.

Eighteen

Fifteen minutes after Logan left, Danni was still pacing the floor, trying to decide exactly what to do — and when to do it. But deep inside her, she knew she had already made her decision. Her cover could be blown at any moment, and she would end up empty-handed, with no story and no way to help Logan. There was simply too much at stake, too much that could go wrong. She must go back. Tonight.

She began to formulate a plan. First, she would go back to her office, turn on the lights, toss some papers around — make it look as though she'd been working.

What if someone saw her on the grounds at this time of night? She shook her head. She could always explain that she had gone home to rest, then come back.

But what if one of the orderlies had found the unlocked window in the infirmary by now and secured it? That was her only way in.

The questions kept coming, each one chipping away at the confidence she needed to go through with this. *Oh, dear Lord, You know I can't do this on my own . . .*

I'll lose my nerve for certain unless I'm sure You're with me. Please get me safely through this night, for Your glory . . . and for Logan. . . .

Nearly an hour later, Danni's confidence had returned, at least for the most part. She had turned on all the lights in her office, booted up her computer, and opened a file on a projected advertising proposal. Her desk was cluttered enough to look as if she had been working for some time.

If anyone had been curious about her presence at this hour of the night, they would have shown up by now. There was no reason to delay any longer. She slipped into her denim jacket, deliberately ignoring the tightness in her chest and the trembling of her hands.

Since it was after curfew, there was no sign of anyone on the grounds. Nevertheless, Danni was thankful for the thick clouds that draped the night in shadows. Her mind raced all the way to the infirmary. She prayed that the window would still be unlocked, that she would recognize the data Logan needed when she found it, that she would find it quickly, that —

Stop it! She drew in a long breath, took a thorough look around the grounds, then pulled the trash barrel under the window and hauled herself up on it.

It was almost a replay of the last time. Relieved to find the window still unlocked, she leaped like a cat onto the floor inside. Quickly she scanned the examining room, then checked out the adjoining waiting room. Except for the furnishings, the room was empty.

She wasted no time in going back to the computer, drumming her fingers while she waited for the system to boot. Her hands were so clammy it was all she could do to type as she entered the same access code as before. The menu appeared, and her eyes traveled down the listings. Except for the "Visitors" file, which she had already copied, she saw nothing else that looked pertinent.

Impatient, she scrolled the menu again, her pulse racing when she saw the words *Geriatric — Inactive.* She highlighted the file, wondering how she had missed it before.

She jumped at the sound of something snapping outside the window and threw the switch to shut down the monitor, so the light wouldn't give her away. She held her breath, getting up and tiptoeing to the window, where she strained to peek out the side without being seen.

There was nothing. After a few seconds more of silence, she trained her flashlight on the floor and crept to the waiting room to look out the front.

Finally satisfied, she hurried back to the computer and restored the screen. This time she didn't hesitate, but immediately opened the highlighted file. It took her only a few seconds to realize what she was seeing as she scrolled through a list of names: *Kendrick, Jennings,* and *Tiergard* flashed onto the screen. Of course! These files had been transferred to an "inactive" status because . . . the men were all dead!

Frantically, she scrolled through page after page of what appeared to be detailed observations, some containing obscure medical terms, on each individual. A number of dated entries appeared to include cryptic references to medication and dosages, along with abbreviated evaluations.

Danni's hands were shaking badly as she fumbled for the blank diskette in her purse, inserted it, and began to copy the document. After the process was complete, she jammed the diskette into a concealed compartment at the bottom of her purse, shut down the system, and exited the building the same way she had entered — through the window.

She beat a frenzied pace back to the *Standard* building, where she collapsed onto her desk chair, shaking so hard she felt bruised. Just as a precaution, since her breath had started coming uneven and labored, she dug her asthma medication out of her purse and placed it on the desk where she could reach it quickly, if necessary. Then she sat, trying to control the violent trembling enough that she could leave the Colony for the last time.

Already the enormous burden of stress she'd been carrying began to drain away a little. Just knowing she would not be coming back to this den of corruption gave her some measure of relief. After tonight, she should have enough pieces of the puzzle to begin developing the exposé. And if the disk in her purse proved to be as informative as she thought it would, she could also help Logan clear his name.

The fleeting thought of Add, her young assistant with the haunted eyes, brought a lump of regret to her throat. She had grown fond of the boy, wished she could have had more time with him, more opportunity to try to help him. Perhaps after this was over and he had learned the truth about Ra and the Colony, he would be more amenable to a different kind of life.

As the shaking finally began to subside, Danni collected a few personal items from her desk, shoving them haphazardly into her briefcase. She waited until last to shut down her computer. Then, with a movement born of habit, she straightened the scattered papers on her desk.

She took one long look around the room, taking grim pleasure in the fact that it would be her *last* look. She had her back to the door and was reaching for the wall switch to turn off the lights when a voice behind her stopped her dead. "More overtime, Sister?"

Danni stiffened, her mind clamoring as she forced herself not to panic. She whipped around to see Ra standing in the doorway. He stepped inside, followed by Penn and the larger of the two orderlies who worked at the infirmary. As the three of them approached, Danni backed up.

Her every instinct was screaming in protest, but she knew her only hope was to keep her composure, stay in control. Obviously, this was no social call.

"You caught me," Danni said, trying for a level tone of voice. "I took a few hours off this afternoon to get some rest. Now I'm paying for it." Danni's smile felt as brittle as glass, but she forced herself to keep it from wavering.

"How very commendable," Ra said smoothly, matching her smile with one of his own. He walked toward her, his floor-length white robe whispering as he moved.

"You know, Sister," he purred, extending one hand outward, palm up, "you are undoubtedly the most dedicated, hardworking employee I've ever had."

He was close enough now for Danni to see that, in contrast to his pleasant, concerned demeanor, his eyes blazed with an unholy rage. "That makes your — termination — even more regrettable."

She refused to cower. "My termination?" she said, meeting his gaze with a cold, level stare.

Flanked by Penn, whose face was a tight mask of anger, and the same orderly who had given Danni the aspirin in the infirmary, Ra stood studying her with what appeared to be clinical curiosity. "Let me correct that, Sister. It is, in fact, *D. Stuart James* we shall be terminating, is it not?"

The roaring in Danni's head increased. She moistened her lips. "I'm afraid I don't understand —"

"Oh, I think you do," Ra quickly contradicted her in a voice thick with menace. "A sharp little newshound like you doesn't miss much, I'm sure."

Knowing any further pretense would be futile, sickly aware that she was trapped, Danni nevertheless made one more try. "Look, I'm really tired," she said firmly, moving as if to skirt Ra and his henchmen. "If it's all right with you, I'll just call it a day and —"

He caught her by the neck so suddenly and so roughly Danni cried out. "Save it," he snarled, the calm, syrupy voice of the *Master Guide* rudely replaced by a new harshness. "You're calling it a day all right, but not in the way you'd intended." He nodded shortly to the orderly. "Take her to the infirmary."

"No!" Danni cried out, trying to twist free. But the big, stone-faced orderly wrested her easily from Ra, locking his burly arms around her middle as he half-dragged her from the room, leaving Ra and Penn to follow behind.

Danni continued to struggle, screaming with all the strength she could muster. They stopped, but only for a moment.

"Shut her up!" grated Ra. The orderly clamped one big hand over Danni's mouth, still holding her securely with his other.

Her lungs screamed for air, and she

choked and coughed, struggling for breath. It was enough to divert the orderly, and he stood unmoving for a moment. She heaved, then again, feeling a stab of sick relief when the precious air filled her lungs and expelled again. Her mind spun as she tried to remember what she had learned from Logan's Karate class.

Danni bit his beefy hand, and, stunned, he yelped and loosened his grip. She managed to free herself from the thick forearm planted around her middle. At the same time, she rammed him with a sharp elbow that knocked him breathless.

But he was a big, rock-hard man, and Danni was too slight — and too inexperienced — to maintain the advantage. The orderly quickly recovered, grasping her in an even tighter hold than before as he pushed her brutally out the door of the *Standard* building and strong-armed her all the way to the infirmary.

Nineteen

As Danni was pushed through the infirmary door and into the glaring light of the examining room, she came as close to hysteria as she had ever been in her life. It was at that moment that she encountered the unblinking stare of Dr. Sutherland.

This man frightened her even more than Ra. And being trapped in the same room with the two of them was enough to take her senses.

Frozen in place, Danni eyed the doctor with cold dread. He stood watching her in a soiled lab coat, both hands clasped in front of him in a gesture that, under the circumstances, seemed obscenely composed.

His mouth thinned to a chilling rictus of a smile. "Help her onto an examining table, please, Curtis."

Danni's heart went crazy, pounding so wildly against her ribs she thought her chest would surely explode. But somehow in the midst of her terror she managed to challenge the orderly. "Take your hands off me!" She jerked, trying to wrestle free of his clutching grasp.

Ra smoothly interposed himself between

Danni and the doctor. "Now, now, Miss St. John — it is *St. John,* isn't it — not *D. Stuart James?* This will go much easier for you if you just cooperate." His tone was indulgent, patently phony, and Danni had never in her life wanted so much to strike a man as she did at this moment.

"No one is going to harm you in any way," he continued, infuriating Danni even more with his benevolent smile. "After all, you're a member of our *family* now."

Something cold and deadening seeped through Danni. "What are you talking about?"

He tilted his head to one side, lifting his brows and widening his eyes in mock surprise. "Why, Sister, you haven't forgotten, have you?"

At Danni's silent glare, he reached out and touched her on the shoulder. Involuntarily, she flinched. "You *have* forgotten! My, you young people today simply *astound* me with your thoughtlessness! It's been only hours since you expressed your desire to disassociate yourself from your old life and join the rest of the family here at the Colony." He gripped her shoulder more tightly.

Danni looked into the glinting, malevolent eyes smiling down at her and knew the most penetrating chill of horror she had ever experienced. "I don't know what you're talking about," she shot back.

His expression remained bland as he moved his hand from her shoulder to lightly pat her cheek. Again, Danni cringed. "Now, don't you worry, Sister. The only thing you're to concern yourself with for the next few hours is getting some much-needed rest. We'll take care of all the necessary arrangements for you to join us."

An ugly, dark suspicion coiled about Danni's mind. "I don't *need* to rest," she rasped out.

"Now, Sister, we've been deeply concerned about you." Ra favored her with a mock frown of concern. "We know all about the long hours you've been working lately, the way you've pushed yourself." He made a clucking sound with his tongue. "I've told you before, dedication is admirable, but you simply must take better care of yourself. Now then," he said firmly, "you just let Curtis help you onto the table. The doctor is merely going to give you a little something to calm your nerves and help you rest."

Danni panicked, straining to free herself. But the orderly was leagues too strong for her. She couldn't shake him. "You're crazy!" she shouted at Ra. "You can't possibly think you're going to get away with this!"

Her outburst was quickly cut off by the orderly's hand over her mouth. "Put her on the table," Ra ordered sharply with a small nod. "And make sure she *stays* there."

In horrified disbelief, Danni felt herself lifted from the floor as if she were a child and carried across the room. The orderly deposited her on one of the white-sheeted examining tables, immediately securing her hands and feet to each side of the frame with heavy cloth restraints.

Through a haze of terror, Danni absorbed only the bare rudiments of what was happening to her. She was seized by the irrational sensation of watching a speeding video, while groping for a switch to turn it off.

She wasn't surprised when she began to wheeze. At first it was no more than a warning shortness of breath. She fought for control, but was so close to losing her grip she could manage only a weak, silent plea for help.

She was only vaguely aware of Penn leaving the room, ordered by Ra to search her office. Danni saw the doctor turn and approach her as her labored breathing grew more noticeable.

Ra, too, watched her, his eyes narrowing with speculation. "What's wrong with her?"

Sutherland assessed her with all the feeling of a butcher gauging a side of beef. "Apparently she's asthmatic." He paused, then added, "Stress often brings on an attack."

Danni turned her head to look when she heard the door open, and, through a blur of bewilderment, she felt a sudden surge of hope. She saw the uniform first, and squeezed her eyes shut against the hot tears of relief. *Logan!*

But when she opened her eyes, she realized that the uniform belonged, not to Logan, but to Philip Rider. Still, he was the law, she consoled herself. Logan was probably right behind him. . . .

And then she saw Rider flash a pointed look at Ra, a look that quickly changed to a lazy, contemptuous smile as he came to stand beside her. She felt a jolt of sick disbelief as she realized just how wrong she had been. In one hand Rider was holding the disk she had copied from the infirmary computer. In the other, which he now lifted like a salute, was her asthma medication. She had forgotten it on her desk.

"I think this is what the lady needs," he drawled, as Danni continued to fight for her breath. He stood over her, passing the medication back and forth in front of her in a playful, taunting gesture.

Danni was almost overcome by a dizzying, blood-freezing fear. She shook her head as if to make the nightmare disappear, but nothing changed. The three of them — Rider, the doctor, and Ra — ringed the table that held her captive, discussing her with seeming indifference to her presence. The enormous circle of light overhead seemed to be shrinking, and the voices around her began to fade. Danni was feeling the lack of oxygen now, knew she would lose consciousness at any moment. She had a sudden, fleeting thought of Logan's face, the look of concern he had worn when she'd last seen him. *Oh, Logan . . . why didn't I listen to you . . . you tried to warn me. . . .*

Somehow, from the depths of the pool in which she was drowning, she saw Rider's smirk become a scowl of disgust. "You've caused a lot of trouble, Miss St. John." He reached across her to hand the medication to the doctor on the other side. "Give her what she needs," he told Sutherland. "Then put her out for the rest of the night. I need some time to go through her house."

He started for the door, then turned back. "Don't let anything happen to her . . . yet," he cautioned the others. "Not until she answers some questions. Just keep her quiet."

He sneered, raking his gaze over Danni. "Honey, you got mixed up with the wrong cop," he said softly. "I could have done you a lot more good than Cousin Logan."

As Philip Rider swaggered out of the room, the doctor released just enough medication into Danni's mouth to help her begin to breath normally. But the relief that washed over her was short-lived, for a few minutes later Sutherland removed a hypodermic syringe from a wall cabinet and started toward her. The last thing Danni realized before the warm, waiting darkness claimed her was that the doctor's hands were shaking even more violently than her own.

Twenty

Across the room, somebody was playing a tape at the wrong speed. Coincidentally, the dragging, slurred voices were in perfect sync with the slow rotation of the circular white light overhead.

Danni wondered dully why her head felt so heavy, why her temples ached with the effort of the slightest movement. There was a treacherous feeling in the pit of her stomach, too . . . and she was weak, too weak to keep her eyes open . . . maybe if she slept, she would feel better. . . .

Her eyelids felt weighted . . . she couldn't keep them open any longer . . . she must be very ill . . . she would sleep awhile . . . maybe she'd feel better later. . . .

But, no, she had to stay awake, had to keep her eyes open, stay alert. She had to listen to the tape . . . the voices on the tape were talking about her. And there was a doctor . . . why? Was she ill? Had Logan called a doctor?

Logan . . . where was Logan?

"Logan?"

The moment she spoke the name, Reverend Ra and the doctor appeared at her side. Danni saw another man, a big, burly man, hunched in a nearby chair.

The orderly!

The fog began to lift from her mind, only to be replaced by a hammer of pain. But she could see more clearly now, and her head didn't feel so heavy, so dull. . . .

"What did she say?"

"She's calling for her boyfriend. McGarey."

Ra sounded angry. He hissed Logan's name as if it were dipped in poison.

"When's Rider coming back? She's coming out of it. Should I put her out again?"

Dr. Sutherland . . . what was he doing here? The man frightened her . . . there was something wrong with him, something terribly wrong. . . .

"No, let her wake up. Rider wants her lucid, so he can question her. He said he'd be back before noon. Keep the restraints on. She's not going anywhere."

In one dead rush, the memory of what had happened came roaring in on Danni. She gasped, somehow managing not to cry aloud as the reality of her situation seized her senses. She squeezed her eyes shut. *They had drugged her . . . she mustn't let them know her mind had cleared . . . she had to think, couldn't panic, had to stay calm. . . .*

"Look, Milo, I don't think —"

"I told you, never call me that here!"

"Sorry," the doctor muttered, his tone resentful. "What do you plan to do with her?"

"How many times do I have to explain?" Ra's voice was harsh with impatience. "You're getting to be as much of a zombie as the rest of these freaks! I'm warning you, Victor, you'd better lay off that garbage. You're no good to me if you can't function."

His words held an unmistakable note of threat. Danni already knew the connection between the two men, where it had begun, why they had joined forces. But she hadn't known about Sutherland's own drug abuse. Not until now.

Danni heard a muffled sound of assent from the doctor before Ra continued, this time in a more mollified tone. "Once Rider's through with her, you can inject her with the same stuff you use for the others. She'll simply meld into the rest of the group. I intend to keep her on the newspaper as long as she's able to function. It won't hurt our image to have it known that a former Christian journalist has left *her* religion for *ours*." He paused, then laughed unpleasantly. "We should be able to get an absolutely *brilliant* editorial from her in support of Hilliard for sheriff!"

Nausea boiled up in Danni's throat. *They would have to kill her first!*

Only sheer strength of will kept her from giving in to hysteria. She forced herself to keep her eyes shut, not wanting them to know she was fully conscious.

". . . and be very sure there are no *accidents* with this one, Victor!"

The doctor actually whined when he answered, "I told you it wasn't my fault. I didn't know they were taking other medication —"

"Oh, save it! Just be sure you know what you're doing this time!"

Dread settled over Danni's chest, threatening to take her breath, but she ground her teeth together and prayed for help.

At the sound of the door slamming, she opened her eyes to see Add. The boy walked in, glanced from the doctor and the orderly to Ra, then to Danni on the examining table. His eyes widened in surprise, and he started toward her. "Miss St. John! What's wrong? What happened?"

Danni saw the doctor grab the boy's arm to stop him. "She's very ill. You can't be in here!"

Ra stepped in at that instant, slipping into

his role as the *Master Guide*. "She'll be fine, Brother Add. But she *does* need medical attention. Unfortunately, our young sister here hasn't yet learned to pace herself. Her dedication to the *Standard* has worn her out." He rested a large hand on the teenager's shoulder, lowering his voice to a conspiratorial murmur. "I'm afraid she's dangerously close to a physical, perhaps even an emotional, breakdown. Dr. Sutherland will be giving her his personal attention. You realize, of course, that while she's ill, we'll be depending on you to keep the paper going for us. We *can* count on you, can't we, son?"

With a troubled expression, the youth darted a look from his leader to Danni. "You can count on me, Reverend Ra. I'll do whatever I can."

Danni took a deep breath and fought to lift her head from the table. "Add! *Help* me!"

A look of alarm washed across the boy's features.

"They're holding me against my will, Add! They drugged me! Call Sheriff McGarey, Add! *Hurry!*"

With his back to the others, the doctor bent over Danni. His face only inches from hers, he ground out a warning. "If you don't shut up, I'll give you an injection you'll *never* come out of."

Add cast a fearful glance her way, then began speaking with Ra in hushed tones. "Reverend Ra, the reason I came to find Dr. Sutherland was to ask what I should do about a vagrant I picked up in the van this morning."

"A vagrant, son?"

"Yes, sir. An elderly man. He was hitch-hiking out on Highway 72 earlier when I went into town to get the kerosene refilled. He nearly fell in front of the van. He's either sick or drunk — I can't tell which."

Ra clucked sympathetically. "We'll have to tend to him, of course. Where is he now?"

"In the parking lot, sir, still in the van. He's conscious, but I think he's delirious or something."

"Well, let's get you some help." Turning to the orderly, Ra beckoned him from his post by the examining table. "This young man needs some assistance with a 'guest' out in the parking lot, Curtis. Would you go with him, please? Bring the poor gentleman inside so the doctor can tend to him."

Danni called Add's name once more before he left, followed by the orderly. But if the boy heard her, he didn't acknowledge it.

When the door opened again, Danni lay

still, lifelessly staring at the ceiling. It was only when she heard Ra grumble, "About time," that she turned to see who had entered the room. She shuddered at the sight of Philip Rider.

He didn't stop until he reached her side. His eyes impaled her as a humorless smile crossed his face. "You have been *very* busy, little lady," he said. As he spoke, he tugged Danni's cassette recorder out of the pocket of his jacket.

Danni's gaze followed the movement, then returned to his face.

He studied her with a look of grim amusement. "I've got to admit, you've got more than your share of nerve." Danni saw then that tucked under his other arm was the folder of photocopied articles and press cards which identified her as *D. Stuart James*. Rider tossed the folder to Ra.

"You might be interested in that, Reverend," he said glibly. "Your new editor probably had big plans for you. I wouldn't be surprised if she didn't intend to put you out of business."

Ra approached the examining table, his eyes flashing. "I know all about it," he said, his voice testy.

Rider's voice hardened. "Then you know that you'll soon be back to selling nonexistent lots in Florida, unless we take care of her, pronto."

"Now, listen here, Rider —"

The deputy's smooth voice cracked like a gunshot. "No, *you* listen. This little Dixie dahlia here has enough information to lock you away." He flashed a furious glare at the doctor. "Thanks to Dr. Frankenstein's sloppy lab records, she knows about Kendrick and the others. And," he paused for effect, "she's got copies of the monthly bank deposits."

"How do you know?"

Rider pulled a crumpled wad of paper from the portfolio. "Apparently she copied some computer data. Here's her own personal printout." He handed the paper to Ra.

The rage on Ra's face after he scanned the printout was enough to make Danni recoil. He bent over her, his features contorted in an ugly, crimson scowl. "You little —"

Rider flung a hand out to restrain Ra. "Save your righteous anger. It's a little late. This babe is trouble — real trouble. You're going to have to deal with her, and the sooner the better. What worries me even more is not knowing just how much she may have told my hard-case cousin."

"McGarey?" For the first time since she'd met the man, Danni saw a look that bordered on fear cross Ra's face.

Rider nodded. "Seems as though they've got a thing going. I have this uncomfortable feeling that Logan may know as much as *she* knows." He turned back to Danni. "What about it, short stuff? Does he?"

Danni hesitated, then shook her head. "He doesn't know anything."

Rider appraised her for several seconds, then gave a nasty smile. "You're lying, lady. I'd bet on it." He whirled around to Ra, who was still hovering nearby. "Logan was to go to Huntsville early this morning. I'm going into town and search his office, see what I can find."

He pointed to Danni over his shoulder. "Make sure she stays right there until I get back. And give her whatever it takes to keep her quiet. I've got to find out what Logan knows. We might have bigger problems than I thought."

He turned on his heel and strode out of the room, leaving Ra standing over Danni with a menacing glare. "Put her out again!" the Colony leader ordered. "And give her enough to shut her up for several hours."

Danni's heart thundered as she watched the doctor go obediently to the supply cabinet and remove a hypodermic syringe and a small vial. Tears of fear and helplessness spilled onto her cheeks.

The door opened just then, and with vast relief she saw Ra motion the doctor to delay the injection for the time being. Add entered first, standing aside to hold the door for the orderly, who was half carrying a disreputable-looking man.

"He's in bad shape, Doc," said the orderly, easily lifting the man off his feet and onto one of the examining tables near Danni. "I think he's sick or something. I don't smell any liquor on him."

Ra stepped in then, donning his serene air of authority, probably for Add's benefit, Danni thought. "Get a blanket for the poor man, Curtis." He wrinkled his nose slightly as he studied the slender form on the table. "And clean him up."

Danni, too, had noticed the man's soiled overalls and hunting jacket. He appeared incredibly filthy. She felt no revulsion, only pity and a stab of fear for whatever fate might await the poor unfortunate.

She looked at Add, who was still standing near the doorway, watching her with a curious expression. She had been foolish, she knew, to hope that he might somehow try to help her. His loyalty was to Ra, and was no doubt too firmly in place by now to shake.

"You can go along now, son," the latter

instructed Add kindly. "We'll take care of this poor gentleman. Did you happen to notice if he has any identification on him, by the way? We need to know if there's someone we should call —"

He turned when the door burst open and Rider charged in, his uniform hat tipped back on his head. He looked harried, Danni noted — harried and angry. "I saw you bringing someone in," he snapped, seemingly unaware of Add's presence. "What's going on?"

Not waiting for a reply, he pushed between the examining tables and stood staring down at the new arrival.

Ra scarcely glanced at the man on the table. "Another derelict, most likely. He seems to be unconscious."

A dark stain spread quickly over Rider's features as he looked up at Ra. "You idiot!"

Ra stepped back, staring at him in astonishment.

"That's no derelict!" Rider shouted. "That's Tucker Wells — Logan's sidekick!"

His words were lost in the din as the "derelict" suddenly dived off the table. At the same time Add flung the door open, and Logan charged into the room like a dark tornado, unleashed and looking for a place to touch down.

Twenty-one

Logan, his gun aimed directly at his cousin, didn't stop moving until he was well into their midst. In his dive from the table, Tucker had hit the orderly full force, just below his knees. A calculated karate punch knocked the wind out of him and sent him sprawling, face down, long enough for Tucker to handcuff him to the metal leg of the computer table.

Danni watched in amazement as Logan, his gun still trained on Philip Rider, threw a precision elbow attack with his free arm at Ra, causing the older man to reel crazily. Tucker, finished with the orderly, grabbed a thick roll of gauze from the utility table and used it to secure Ra to a chair before heading for the doctor.

Sutherland, however, had grabbed the hypodermic syringe he'd filled earlier. Before either Logan or Tucker could reach her, the doctor clamped a hand around Danni's throat, nearly choking off her air. "I'll kill her!" he screamed wildly, waving the syringe over Danni's head like a madman. "Just stop where you are, or she's dead, I'm warning you!"

Logan, pivoting so as to keep Rider in his sights, appraised the hysterical doctor. Tucker stopped dead in his tracks, a few feet from the disabled Ra, squinting from Logan to Sutherland.

"All right . . . all right, now . . ." babbled the doctor, his face bathed in perspiration, his eyes glassy. "Add —" everyone looked at the boy standing quietly by the door — "you get the sheriff's gun and bring it to me."

The boy blinked, hesitated, then started toward Logan.

"Don't do it, son," Tucker said quietly as Add passed him.

But Add went on, not stopping until he reached Logan. The two of them locked gazes for a long moment before the boy extended a trembling hand, palm upward, for the gun. Danni's hopes plummeted when she saw Logan hand the gun over without a word.

"That's fine, boy," the doctor babbled as Add took the gun to him. "Bring it here, now, that's fine."

Add didn't so much as glance at Danni as he approached, instead walked around the side of the examining table to Sutherland.

Suddenly, in a lightning-fast move, Add threw himself against the doctor, thrusting the gun into Sutherland's abdomen and flinging out one long arm to knock the hypodermic from his hand.

At the same time, Logan moved, hurling himself into a spinning storm of assault against Rider. He high-kicked the other's service revolver out of his hand, and with two deadly accurate punches, sent his cousin reeling over a chair.

Tucker grabbed Rider's gun and, moving incredibly fast for a man with a lame leg, rocketed past Danni to help Add pin the doctor against the wall.

"You did just fine, son," Tucker panted. "Now, help the lady out of those restraints," he instructed the boy, pressing the gun under Sutherland's nose.

Add seemed close to weeping as he struggled to free Danni. "Are you all right, Miss St. John? I'm sorry — I'm so sorry I couldn't help you when I was here the first time! The sheriff made me promise not to do anything — he said I should find you and make sure the door was unlocked!" His words tumbled out as he loosed the last restraint. The instant Danni was free, she sat up and gave him an enormous hug.

"Oh, Add! You *did* call Logan, after all!"

"No, ma'am. The sheriff called *you,* early this morning. He called your office, and when I told him you hadn't come in yet, he said you weren't at home either, and asked me to check on you, said to find you and call him back."

"But when you were here earlier —"

The boy's words continued to spill from his lips in a torrent. "I told him what they'd done to you — what I saw — and Sheriff McGarey, he told me exactly what to do. He explained that his friend, Mr. Wells, would meet me on the road, that he'd be dressed like a vagrant, and that I should bring him here and then just wait."

"Danni? Are you all right?" Logan shouted across the room as he handcuffed the doctor to an examining table.

"I'm okay!"

After sending Add out to the patrol car to radio for the state police, Logan and Tucker cuffed Philip Rider.

Only then did he turn to Danni, and the riot of conflicting emotions marching across his features made her catch her breath. She closed the distance between them, would have thrown herself at him in grateful relief, but stopped when she saw his eyes.

"Get your story, Half-pint?" he growled.

"Logan —" She glanced from him to Tucker, who shrugged, then grinned and walked away.

It was anyone's guess what was going on

inside Logan's head, but to Danni he looked for all the world like a hurricane about to roll.

"Would you concede that maybe you got a little carried away with the *courage of your convictions?*" he snarled.

He was *angry* with her! Would she *ever* understand this man? "You're *angry?*" she exploded. "I was minutes away from being turned into a vegetable, or . . . or maybe even murdered . . . and you decide to *lecture* me? Now you wait just one minute, Logan McGarey —"

The look he turned on her almost sent Danni to her knees. "No, *you* wait a minute!" he roared. "We are not having this conversation right now. I hurt my back. I have just been scared out of ten years of my life. I risk my own neck and a perfectly good patrol car, burning up the road to get out here before these dirt bags turn your brain to mush — or worse —" He stopped, dropping his voice only a little as he added, "Yes, ma'am, you might say I'm *angry!*"

He left Danni standing there with her mouth open as he crossed the room to where Philip Rider lay, sprawled and handcuffed to the sink. As furious as she was with Logan at that moment, Danni couldn't stop a twinge of sympathy for him when she saw the hurt that settled over his features as he stood studying the cousin who had betrayed him.

"I thought you were going to Huntsville," Rider muttered, his look surly.

"That's what you were supposed to think." Logan paused. "How deep are you in, Phil? And why? What possessed you to get mixed up in this?"

The younger man glared at Logan defiantly, his mouth set in an obstinate pout. "Why *not?*" he shot back contemptuously. "Not all of us are as high-minded as you . . . *Cousin.*"

"What's that supposed to mean?"

"It means *money,* man! A lot of money. Something you and the rest of our tribe wouldn't know anything about."

Danni saw Logan's jaw tighten even more. His face looked to be carved in granite as he went on questioning Rider. "What part did you play in this? And tell me the truth. I've had enough of your lies."

Rider managed a bravado shrug. "Protection, mostly. I just made sure no one caught on to the welfare scam, covered their tracks when they got careless —"

Logan didn't let him finish. "Let's see if I've figured it out: the kids brought in vagrants who didn't have anywhere else to go.

After a few doses of Dr. Sutherland's magic potion, the old guys signed their welfare checks over to the Colony, and from then on they were kept happily drugged and out of the way. Only the ones without family — at least family who *cared* about them — were encouraged to stay. Right?"

Rider looked at him. "How'd you find out about the welfare checks?"

"I made a couple of trips to the Social Security office in Huntsville," Logan said, his tone chillingly hard. "So what about the three men who died?"

Again Rider shrugged. But this time he dropped his gaze away from Logan's fierce stare. "The *doctor* over there said they must have been taking some other kind of medication that reacted to the zombie juice he mixed up special for them. Something happened to their hearts, I guess."

Add had come back into the room and was talking quietly with Tucker during this exchange. Danni went to stand a little closer to Logan, but he gave no sign that he was aware of her presence.

"Why did you search Danni's house? And how many times — once . . . twice?"

Rider's gaze turned scornful. "What makes you think *I* did that?"

Logan reached down to his cousin's shirt

pocket and pulled out a pair of sunglasses, turning them over a few times, then holding them up to the light as he studied them. Finally, he retrieved something from his own pocket — the small piece of metal Danni had found in her lingerie drawer. He placed it beside the temple of the sunglasses in his hand, where a piece of tape had been wrapped, apparently to cover a missing part.

"I knew there was something familiar about this," he said, "but I couldn't connect it until I noticed that piece of tape on your sunglasses yesterday."

He lifted a hand and gingerly stroked a bruise on his cheek. Danni ached to touch the bruise herself, but the look she had seen in his eyes a few minutes before stopped her.

"It was you who marked up Penn and harassed Otis Green, wasn't it?" he said, his tone more harsh now.

Rider shot his cousin a belligerent look. "I didn't hurt them — just roughed Penn up a little."

"I thought Green's change of heart was a little too quick," Logan said. "What did you threaten him with — jail?"

Rider nodded.

"And they *agreed* to letting you rough them up!"

"They didn't have any choice," Rider said, his tone edged with disdain. "Their illustrious *Master Guide* made it clear that it was all in the best interests of the Colony."

Logan turned toward Ra, almost bumping into Danni, who glared up at him with a silent demand that he notice her. Instead, he looked right over her head. "Tell me, *Reverend Ra,*" he said caustically, "what's your real name?"

"Milo Cavendar," inserted Danni quickly.

Logan looked down at her, studying her face for what seemed like a very long time. Finally, one dark brow quirked, and Danni was pretty sure he was tempted to smile. He didn't, of course. *Brave Eagle* would never smile in the face of the enemy.

"Milo Cavendar," he repeated.

"That's right. I do my homework before I take an assignment. He's also known as *Floyd Basil, Leonard Sprague,* and *Stanley Coates.*"

Tucker and Add had walked over and now stood listening quietly. Again touching the bruise on his cheek, Logan's gaze drifted over Danni. She knew she probably looked like something out of a bad dream.

But at least she had his attention now. "He's been a securities salesman, a real estate developer, and a smut peddler. And that just covers the last ten years."

Both eyebrows lifted this time, and, yes, there was definitely the faint glimmer of a smile. In fact, his whole expression was gentling, warming to the familiar glint of amused tolerance and tender affection that could make her heart race like a wild thing.

She pressed on. "He's been arrested twice for fraud, once for credit card counterfeiting, and has a whole sheet of traffic tickets on file." Feeling pretty good now, Danni decided to wrap it up. "He used to fight pit bulls, too."

When she saw Logan's mouth drop slightly open and that wonderful, sweet softness dawn in his eyes, she decided to go for the jugular. *"And —"*

He groaned. "You're really something, aren't you?"

". . . he's part Indian." Silence. "Like you."

Luckily for Danni, Deputy Baker and two state troopers came hurrying through the door at that moment.

Twenty-two

"Hard to believe it'll soon be Christmas," Tucker commented later that same evening as he refilled their cups with his coffee. "Want some more hot chocolate, son?" he asked Add. The boy was sitting directly across the table from Danni, dividing his attention between his new friends and the Irish setter puppies scampering back and forth.

"Well, in case anyone's interested, I've already got *my* present," Danni said with a bright smile, glancing down at her feet where Chief, a fat and shiny ball of copper fur, was busily trying to bite his own tail. Sassy, his mother, rested quietly on the other side of Logan, occasionally giving her incorrigible pups a maternal warning growl.

Tucker had insisted on everyone going out to the farm as soon as Logan and the state troopers herded their prisoners into town. They had already devoured a delicious meal — prepared by Tucker — of baked ham, browned potatoes, and cornbread, and Danni was now on her third brownie.

"What's going to happen to all those people out at the Colony now?" Tucker asked Logan, returning to the table.

Logan took another sip of coffee and inclined his head toward Danni, seated beside him. "She thinks she's got it all figured out," he said dryly.

Tired as she was, Danni couldn't curb her enthusiasm. "I'm going to contact the local churches and see if they'll help. The grounds and the facilities would make a perfect shelter for troubled teens. And I'll just bet that a lot of those elderly people would thrive on the responsibility of helping to take care of the young people and the property. Of course, for those who might not want to stay, we'll try to find homes."

"I'd enjoy helping out with the young people," Tucker offered. "I have a fondness for teenagers." He smiled at Add, and the boy gave him a shy look of gratitude in return.

"What do you intend to use for money?" asked Logan, ever the cynic.

"The Colony coffers," Danni replied. "The courts will have to administer the funds, but there must be a considerable amount tied up in banks all over the state. That will give us a good start, and if we can get some support from the churches later — it will work. I know it will."

Logan leaned back in his chair, his arms

crossed over his chest. "I don't think you'll have much of a problem getting them to pitch in."

Danni looked at him in surprise. "You *don't?*"

He shook his head. "No. I think that when they finally realize what's been going on out there, they'll want to help."

Danni studied him. "That's a switch for you, isn't it? Giving the churches the benefit of the doubt?"

He shrugged. "I suppose it is. I'm beginning to think I might have expected too much in the beginning, before we really knew for certain what the Colony was up to. Once the people in town learn the truth, I think they'll help."

He watched Danni warily, as if half expecting her to challenge this change of heart. When she didn't, he went on. "Let's just say you helped to restore my faith in human nature, Half-pint. At least you made me realize that some people *do* put legs on their faith. That's a start for me." He smiled. "By the way, I found those missing articles of yours."

Danni frowned. "What articles?"

"The clippings from your mother's scrapbook," he explained. "The ones that had been removed, remember?"

"Oh! Where were they? *What* were they?"

His eyes held hers. "Phil had them. And what they were," he added pointedly, "were articles about a journalism award. For *investigative reporting.*"

Danni twisted her mouth. "Oh . . . *those* articles."

He shook his head. With his next question, his mood seemed to turn more solemn. "So . . . are you planning to stay around Red Oak? To help out with the transition out at the Colony?"

His words were impersonal enough, but something in his tone made Danni think . . . *hope* . . . that her answer might be important to him.

She looked at him, saw that *Brave Eagle*'s defenses appeared to be down . . . at least for the moment. "I . . . I'm in no hurry to leave," she said, hastening to add that she would probably stay in Red Oak while she was writing the story. "And I wouldn't mind helping out at the Colony — we need to give that place a new name, don't you think — they're going to need a lot of help —"

She broke off, suddenly aware that she was chattering. She gave him a lame smile. "Well . . . I'll be staying for a while, yes."

She was only vaguely aware when Tucker cleared his throat and rose from the table.

"Jerry," he said, calling Add by his given name, "I could use some help in the kitchen, if you wouldn't mind."

Danni smiled as Add — *Jerry* — practically tripped over himself getting up. He started to follow Tucker out of the room when Logan stopped them.

"Tucker?"

Tucker turned back, waiting.

"Many thanks, *kemo sabe,*" Logan said quietly.

The look that passed between them brought a catch to Danni's throat.

She and Logan sat in silence for what seemed an interminable time. Finally, Logan, in an obvious attempt to make conversation, said, "Tucker would like the boy to stay on with us for a while. I told him it was fine with me."

"Oh, Logan, I'm so glad! Add — Jerry — has real promise. He's a good kid, really. He just needs someone to care about him and give him some guidance."

Logan nodded. "We'll enjoy having him around. Tucker's great with young people. He's a youth counselor at his church, you know. He's helped to straighten out more than one mixed-up kid over the years. The boy could do worse than have Tucker as a friend."

"And you," Danni said softly, watching him.

He glanced away for a moment, then turned back. "There's something I need to say to you."

Danni's heart began to race.

"I just wanted to tell you that I'm sorry, for the way I yelled at you earlier today."

It wasn't what she had hoped to hear, and Danni had to work at concealing her disappointment. "Yes . . . well, you certainly did put me in my place," she said lightly.

"I was scared," he admitted. "It's one thing to preach about 'getting involved,' but when someone you . . . care about . . . is the one on the line, it's different. I hope that's not a double standard, but the truth is, I acted like a bear because I was just plain terrified. And once I knew you were all right —" He shrugged and gave her an uncertain smile. "Well, I just wanted to explain."

Not trusting her voice, Danni simply nodded that she understood. With a sinking feeling, she knew it was time for her own confession. She swallowed, moistened her lips, and began. "Logan, I hope you won't be too upset with me about this — I mean, now that you know the reason for my taking the job at the Colony — but I have to tell you something."

She told him then about the evening with Ra — Milo Cavendar. Anxious to get what was almost certain to be another explosion over and done with, she admitted that what she had hoped to accomplish hadn't materialized, that she had instead been humiliated, and that she deeply regretted her actions.

Logan's expression grew darker and darker throughout the narrative, until at last, when Danni had finally finished the entire story — complete with a plea for his understanding — he looked like he might start tearing up the room around them. "Logan — it was a mistake, I knew that almost as soon as I walked in," Danni insisted. "It was a foolish risk, and I would never, never do something that rash again!"

She held her breath, watching him. It occurred to her that perhaps he didn't *care* that she had spent the evening alone with a sleazy con man. But if that were the case, what accounted for his murderous expression?

Finally, he jerked to his feet, and without a word, left the room. With his exit, the bottom dropped out of Danni's heart. She had anticipated a chastising, even another tirade. Anything but this awful silence.

Well, why should she have expected anything else? Even before tonight, he had already thought she was the worst kind of a fool. Now he was convinced of it. She should have known this would happen. And she could hardly blame him.

She supposed there was nothing she could do, except leave . . . get out of his life.

She bit her lip in an effort to keep from weeping. At that moment Logan strode back into the room, his face an impassive mask.

Without warning, he pulled Danni to her feet and with one smooth, precise move — handcuffed her wrist to his!

"What are you *doing?*" Danni burst out.

His expression never changed as he lifted her hand a little to check the lock on the cuffs. "Arresting you," he said mildly.

"Arrest—" Danni gaped at him. "Logan McGarey, you take these things off me right now, do you hear me?" she demanded. "This is not funny!"

"Breaking and entering," he said as if he hadn't heard her, "is against the law. My job requires me to arrest you."

"Ohhh!" Danni twisted, trying to pull free of him, but succeeded only in wrenching her wrist. "What are you talking about — breaking and entering?"

She knew exactly what he was referring

to, of course. The infirmary.

"For your information, Logan, I broke into the infirmary as much for *you* as for me!"

Somehow her effort to break free had only served to close the distance between them. "I'm not talking about the infirmary," he said in that exasperating monotone.

"Then, *what?* What's this nonsense about *arresting* me?"

He tugged her closer, his features still unreadable, although Danni thought she detected a glint in his eye that hadn't been there before. With his free arm, he gathered her into a secure embrace, leaving their handcuffed wrists to dangle uselessly at their sides. "I have decided," he said matter-of-factly, looking down at her, "that you are dangerous. You broke into my heart. You just walked in and took over, stole my heart and got away with it before I even knew what hit me. Now, I'm just a thick-headed cop, not a lawyer, but even I know that could easily be construed as breaking and entering. So . . . I'm arresting you."

With her pulse doing a step-dance, Danni had all she could do to show as much restraint as her captor. "I believe I'm entitled to a trial," she pointed out.

He seemed to consider her words.

"That's true," he said. "But I have to tell you that it will go a lot easier for you if you plea bargain and get it over with."

"What kind of a sentence are we discussing?"

He drew her even closer, pressing a light kiss to the top of her head. "Well, I'm a pretty good friend of the judge. If you accept my terms, I can probably get you off with life."

"In your custody?"

"Didn't I mention that?"

Danni reached with her free hand to gently touch his bruised cheek. "In that case," she said, "I accept."